Over the Line

Over the Line

DAVID LLOYD

Syracuse University Press

∞ The paper used in this publication meets the minimum requirements of the
American National Standard for Information Sciences—Permanence of Paper for
Printed Library Materials, ANSI Z39.48-1992.

For a listing of books published and distributed by Syracuse University Press, visit our
website at SyracuseUniversityPress.syr.edu.

ISBN: 978-0-8156-1022-9

Library of Congress Cataloging-in-Publication Data
Lloyd, David T., 1954–
    Over the line / David Lloyd. — First edition.
        pages cm
    ISBN 978-0-8156-1022-9 (pbk. : alk. paper) 1. Teenage boys—Fiction. 2. High
schools—Fiction. 3. School violence—Fiction. 4. Life change events—Fiction.
I. Title.
    PS3612.L57O84 2013
    813'.6—dc23   2013017578

Manufactured in the United States of America

For my brother
Gareth Aeron Lloyd
(1941–2001)

Fiction writer, poet, and critic **David Lloyd** directs the Creative Writing Program at Le Moyne College in Syracuse, NY. He is the author of eight books, including a fiction collection (*Boys: Stories and a Novella*, from Syracuse University Press [2004]) and three poetry collections. His most recent poetry collection, *Warriors*, was published by Salt Publishing in 2012. His stories and poems have appeared in numerous journals, including *Crab Orchard Review*, *Denver Quarterly*, *Planet*, and *Stone Canoe*. In 2000, he received the Poetry Society of America's Robert H. Winner Memorial Award, judged by W. D. Snodgrass.

Contents

Acknowledgments

I WANT TO THANK the following people for reading the manuscript and giving valuable advice: Steven Chudney, Patrick Lawler, Margaret Lloyd, Linda Pennisi, Richard Russo, Patrick Scully, and Kim Waale. I am indebted to my editor at Syracuse University Press, Deanna McCay, for her enthusiastic and efficient support. For providing time for writing and revising, I am grateful to the Blue Mountain Center, which awarded a writing residency, and to Le Moyne College, which granted a sabbatical leave.

In Chapter 11 I quote from William Shakespeare's *The Tragedy of Macbeth* (5.5.25–30).

Over the Line

1

Sunday

I WAS ON MY WAY to the fridge for a soda when I saw something through the front window that made me stop and stare: a skinny girl walking, and sometimes stumbling, down the middle of our street. That would be strange to see at any time, but especially on a Sunday afternoon, and especially in my neighborhood. She was wearing jeans and a flannel shirt with the tail hanging out. Her greasy black hair, parted in the middle, fell around her hunched shoulders. She stopped, for no reason I could figure out, exactly in front of our house. Walking or standing, she kept her shoulders hunched, like she had to protect her skinny neck. I thought about calling Dad, but could hear him talking upstairs on the phone, so I just kept an eye on her through the window. When she looked around, first away from me but then toward me, I knew who she was: a spooky girl from school named Vera Knight, Del Blake's girlfriend—a girl who didn't live anywhere near me.

A Ford Focus slowed to a stop behind Vera and honked once—old Mrs. Abbott, a neighbor from down the street driving to her daughter's house as she did every Sunday. Vera turned, and lazily stuck out and lifted her middle finger. The car slowly crept in a wide circle around Vera. Mrs. Abbott never did anything fast—walking, talking, or driving—and she obviously wanted to keep her distance. I couldn't blame her for that. I could see her old-lady head gawking as she drove. After ten or so more halting steps Vera turned, checked around herself, and started back the way she'd just come. Then she really stumbled—like she'd tripped on air, or like someone had cut the invisible strings holding her up—and fell to her hands and knees on the pavement. That had to hurt. I thought she'd just stand back up, brush herself off, and keep staggering. Instead, she stayed down on all fours, like a dog too exhausted to move.

———

"You OK?" I asked.

She jerked her head up then scanned around, as if looking for a place to crawl to, and I saw a wet, yellow-brown stain down the front of her shirt. I breathed in a sour whiff of beer and vomit.

"I said, are you OK?"

This time she looked directly at me, squinting.

"You're in my school, right? Your name's Vera. I've seen you around."

She dropped her head, then raised it up, which I guess meant "yes." When she finally spoke, the words were slow and slurred. "Where . . . am I?"

"Erie St. You know, in East Liberty."

"Where's . . . the car?"

"What car?"

She stood up awkwardly. "Del's. They . . . dumped me."

"Because you got sick?"

She did her droopy-head nod. Her shirt sleeve was ripped at the elbow, and a grass stain covered most of one pant leg. Could Del and his friends really have thrown her out of a car because she got sick?

"Those guys," she said. She laughed, loud and sharp, more a cough than a laugh. "Those guys. Assholes. They shoot squirrels. They snort and shoot and snort. Makes my nose burn. But squirrels are fast." She laughed again. "Squirrels jump."

"Yeah," I said, not knowing what else to say. "They can jump all right."

She lifted her hands, studied one palm then the other, and held out both for me to look at.

"Jesus," I said, "you're bleeding. You skinned your hands."

Then she did a strange thing. She licked her palm from the base to the top of her middle finger and held the hand in front of her mouth as she considered the taste. She winced. She pulled her hands into fists at her sides.

"They hurt," she said.

"Yeah, you need to clean them up."

"You," she said.

Suddenly she could focus, and looked me directly in the eyes.

"Why? Why you, anyways?"

"Me?"—I didn't like how she suddenly got personal. "What did I do?"

"Why do you see me?" she said loudly. "What's to see?"

"I don't know what you're saying."

"Tell me why. Why they dumped me."

"I wasn't there. I don't know."

"You know," she said.

"I *don't* know." I felt like I was talking to a four-year-old. A four-year-old with really slurred speech. Why should I know what psychos in a car are thinking? And what was I supposed to do about it?

"The road," she said.

"What?"

"Where's . . . the road?"

"You mean Route 8?"

She nodded.

"Straight ahead, first right, then the next left."

I realized this was too much information for her to absorb.

"It's a five-minute walk. Is that where they dumped you? Route 8? Is that where you walked from?"

"Yeah, the road. Where's the road?"

That's when I understood I didn't have a choice about what to do.

"Come in the house," I said. I took a deep breath. "That's the best thing. My dad's home. Come in and use the phone. I live there." I pointed behind me. "Your dad could pick you up and take you home."

In fact I'd never seen or heard anything about Vera's parents, though we lived in a small town. It was as if she didn't have any. Or brothers or sisters.

"Bandages," she said. "For my head." She laughed. "I need them."

"Your head? You hurt your head?"

She laughed again—a loud cackle-laugh. "It's all busted up in there," she said. "A bazillion pieces. I'm whacked in there." Then she turned and lurched away, zigzagging down the middle of the street, faster this time. She didn't look back.

When she'd followed the curve of the road out of my sight, I ran up the steps to my front door, opened it, and stood for a few seconds in the doorway, looking back at the empty street.

It felt good to get away from that creepy girl, her creepy problems, her nauseating smells. I could hear Dad still on the phone in the upstairs hall. I thought about what might happen next. Either Vera would get lost again, and maybe in her confusion end up staggering back to my street, or else she'd find Route 8, and then what? Maybe stagger down the middle of it, flipping off cars, until someone speeding around a blind curve would slam into her—that road had lots of blind curves and no one obeyed the speed limit.

I walked to the kitchen and found a soda in the fridge—the last ginger ale—and sat on a chair. I tried to remember what TV shows would be on after dinner. Then my mind went blank, and I leapt up and took off out the front door, jumping the steps in one leap, running after Vera. Just as I caught sight of Route 8, I stopped to catch my breath. And there she was at the roadside getting into a car—an old Pontiac Grand Prix. She sort of fell into the back seat, an arm yanked the door shut, and the car sped off.

———————

Back in the house Dad was off the phone. I was going to run up to tell him about Vera, but just stood at the bottom of the stairs, thinking.

Dad isn't the type who can let things go. He likes to hang on. He'd get this concerned furrow in his brow, purse his lips, then come up with lots of questions, so I'd end up telling him everything. He'd press for details. He'd need to find out where she lived and phone her family. He'd ask if I knew who was driving the car. A man or woman? Or was it boys in the car? How old were they? He'd want to drive up and down Route 8 looking for the car to make sure Vera was OK. If she wasn't OK, he'd need to do something about that. He might even call our town cop Jack Boland to tell him what happened. He'd want to do something because a drunk girl who'd been snorting up, wandering alone on a Sunday afternoon in our neighborhood, just wasn't right. And Dad needs things to be right.

It didn't sit right with me either, it's true, but if I told my dad anything, this wouldn't end with Vera getting driven away. It would go on . . . and on and on.

2

Sunday

ON SUNDAYS BEFORE DINNER Dad and I always took the same walk: along Route 8 for a mile or so, then back. As usual, Dad was walking fast along the roadside—no sidewalks out there—taking long strides, so I had to work to keep up even though I'm almost as tall as him. He was in full talking mode. Enrollment at the community college was down because young people were leaving East Liberty. They were leaving because farms and businesses were moving south or west, or going bankrupt: the brewery, the sawmill a few weeks after that, the candle factory, the meat packing plant three months later, then the Marietta plant, when Mom left, though Dad didn't mention Mom. Mom is always around, and never around.

"And what's going up on the corn fields?" Dad said. "Walmart, that's what. And junk housing. Cookie cutter developments or McMansions sprouting like . . ." he couldn't get the words but finally came out with, " . . . like cold sores."

"Thanks for putting that image in my mind, Dad."

"Well, it's true. Not pretty, but true. And who are these people, anyway? Who's moving into those mini-mansions? You never see them in the downtown stores, or what's left of downtown. Where'd they come from? Are they invisible? Where do they work to make all their money? Why do they want to live next to us? And why do they need to be lords of the manor? You know what Jack Boland calls that kind of house?"

"What?"

"A parachute palace."

"Why?"

"Looks like a plane dropped it out of the sky."

The junk developments and parachute palaces I could do without, but I wasn't sure about Walmart. At least Walmart might have jobs after high school for guys like Rusty Taylor or Fred Gardiner or Donny Schill. It's a place where bankrupt farmers could buy shingles to patch up their roofs now that Hartnett's Hardware had closed. Where they could find cheap clothes for their kids. Where old people could get coffee and a slice of pizza. Jesus, Dad, it's not so easy! I said to myself.

There was a new McMansion in a field on the left—part of the old Osbourne farm. The Osbournes kept their farmhouse, the barn, and three acres, and sold the rest. We'd watched the McMansion get built during our Sunday walks, with Dad commenting on each phase. "I heard the owner's a Syracuse lawyer," Dad said. "He must have paid hundreds of thousands to build that thing. But it's cheap. Cheap masquerading as expensive, fake pretending to be real. Everyone's supposed to be fooled."

The "beautiful" chimney was an inch of fake stone over concrete blocks, with prefab units trucked in for the insides of the house. It was strange to see it finished, with eight little roofs, a three-car garage, a row of trimmed bushes along the walk to the front door. No real trees; just spick-and-span boulders plunked here and there. Boulders without a speck of moss.

"Remember Hartnett's?" I asked.

"Of course," Dad said. "That closed last year, didn't it?"

"And remember that old guy who sat in the folding chair outside the front door, drinking from a bottle in a paper bag?"

"George Andrews." Dad laughed. "George had something of a drinking problem."

"So Hartnett let him get drunk outside his store? And the cops ignored it? Isn't that illegal?"

Dad thought about this. "George never bothered anyone. He was always polite. He just didn't have anywhere to go. He sat outside that store ever since I can remember—he'd been friends with Hartnett's father. He liked watching people come and go while he drank his Mogen David. Nodding hello, nodding good-bye. His major problem was getting himself up out of that chair to have a pee in Hartnett's toilet, then finding his way down the aisle to the chair without wrecking the place. Remember how packed Hartnett's shelves used to be?"

"What happened to him anyway? When the store shut down he just disappeared."

"I don't know," Dad said. "Where does a guy like that go? A guy who can hardly get up out of a chair."

We walked a while without talking. And as we walked, my eyes followed the road edge, where ahead of us, half on the road, half on the grass, lay a dead squirrel, legs splayed as if he was swimming. His grayish fur was weirdly matted, though it hadn't rained for a week. A trail of blood led from his mouth into the grass, but his ears and paws were small and delicate, like on a stuffed toy. Something had pulled an eye out from the empty red socket. A crow maybe. Or turkey vulture. His tail was missing. That was odd, I thought. What kind of scavenger eats just the tail? Because he was on his side, I could see the white fuzz of his underbelly—and a little black hole, a pellet gun hole.

We reached the stretch of road bordered by one of the really old tumble-down stone walls you see on upstate roads, held together by gravity and luck, since they didn't use cement. It was late September, but would be warm the whole week, Indian summer before the real cold settles around East Liberty. Already the leaves along Route 8 were turning orange, red, and gold, and farmers had cut their corn down to yellow stalks. The roadsides were crammed with black-eyed Susans and milkweed: Mom taught me those names—along with the name of every bird in our neighborhood—back when she came along on our walks.

Then I blurted out the question on my mind that's always lurking in some corner, no matter what I'm doing.

"Dad, why did Mom leave?"

He looked at me, surprised to hear that question on a Sunday walk. "We've talked about this, Justin. You know why. Gerald. Because of Gerald."

"Gerald isn't so great. I don't get Gerald."

Dad smiled. "The truth is," he said, "your mother thinks I'm not as"—he paused—"not as demonstrative as she'd like."

"So Gerald is Mr. Demonstrative?"

"Apparently."

"Can I call him that next time I see him?"

"No, you can't."

"OK," I said. "So go on."

"I love your mother. Showing it was the problem. I mean, showing it in ways she noticed. Or that . . . that were possible for me. Your mother needed something different than I could give." Dad shook his head. "And, of course, there was little Mike. That was . . . well, you know that was hard."

Dad wasn't smiling now. His shoulders slumped, his pace slowed. My brother Michael died in his crib, just two months old. You'd think losing a child might bring a family closer, not break it apart. I didn't think Dad understood what went wrong in his marriage any more than me. I'm not even sure my mom knew what went wrong. It involved Gerald, but it was bigger than him. Even bigger than losing little Mike. Poor Dad, I thought. Mom still says "I love you" to me, but not to him. He must sometimes sit down and wonder, how the hell did *that* happen?

Up ahead I saw a car turn slowly onto our road at the top of the hill. Dad didn't notice because he'd retreated deep into his head. It's familiar territory. As an English professor he spends a lot of time in there.

When Dad started up again about him and Mom, my eyes were on the car, snaking left and right. It never crossed the center line, or veered too near the roadside ditch. But whoever was driving wasn't driving too well.

"I'm better at talking about feelings than I used to be," Dad said. "Better, but not there yet. The other thing is, your mother's so much younger. And it didn't help that she was my student when we met. It's just how things were back then."

I saw that the approaching car was the same blue Grand Prix that had picked up Vera. Now I knew why the driving was so bad. I counted two heads in the front, two in back.

"Of course it would have been better if she hadn't worked at Marietta. Maybe she'd have gotten her master's in botany, though I don't know what job she'd have found. Seen any greenhouses in East Liberty? Still, it's a shame we never . . ."

As the Grand Prix passed, a hand holding a McDonald's super-size cup popped out the open window and doused my father, who shouted "What?" and stopped in his tracks. Dad was a perfect shield—not a drop touched me. A voice from the car yelled, "Gotcha!" followed by hoots and war cries. "What the . . . Good Christmas . . . Jesus Jacob . . ." Dad sputtered, as close to swearing as he gets. He swung around, staring at the car roaring off, horn blasting.

"ACT 236!" he shouted, pointing at the disappearing car. "ACT 236, can't get the rest. Remember. Blue. ACT 236, New York plate. Could have killed someone."

Dad ran a hand over his cardigan. "Soaked. Completely soaked." He sniffed his hand. "Is this what I think it is?"

I leaned in and sniffed. "Yuck. Piss."

"I can't believe it," Dad said. "Disgusting. Those were boys your age or not much older, right? Had to be. And drunk or on drugs, or both. Did you recognize them?"

"No."

Of course I knew that car, and everyone in it. Del Blake driving, Tommy DeSantis next to him—Del's a year older than me but failed a grade, which is why he could drive while only a sophomore. Vera Knight sat in the back, next to the hulking football player Will Hayes. I thought it was strange that Del didn't let his girlfriend sit with him.

Dad took off the cardigan, held it by its neck, and we turned to walk home. We didn't talk all the way back because Dad was stewing. Ruminating. Cogitating. Taking his own walk inside his head, a long one. At our front door he turned to me.

"Those are kids without principle. They see two people on a pleasant Sunday walk and say to each other, let's throw urine at them. Where's the sense in that?"

I could have told Dad the truth: they had a lame principle, which was: trash what you don't like, especially if you've drunk five or six beers, and smoked however many joints, and snorted however much you were snorting. At some point somebody pissed in that super-size cup—OK, that's plenty weird but all that beer had to go somewhere. Once the pissing was done, they needed something on the road that begged to be doused. Maybe they remembered the "No Bush No War" election sign Dad had planted in our front yard, when almost everyone in this town supported the war, or "supports the troops," whatever that means—the sign lasted three days before someone stole it. Maybe they didn't like the looks of Dad, or his stupid sweater. Maybe they didn't like the nonentity that was me.

Or maybe it was because I wasn't exactly a nonentity. Del and I had been friends when he was eleven and I was ten—a friendship that's hard to imagine now. Back then I got on a school bus that went down Bishop St. to pick up Del, who'd sit by himself towards the front. One morning when someone had taken Del's usual seat, he walked down the aisle and sat across from me. After fishing around in a canvas sack he used for a book bag, he pulled out a dog-eared paperback, like something from a garage sale or someone's trash. A rubber band held the thing together. I'd never seen anyone on that bus read a book besides me. At some point he said "hi," and I said "hi." And we talked across the aisle about what we were reading. I don't remember the title of my book, but it was a hardcover and thicker than Del's. When the bus arrived at school, he reached in his pocket and offered me a quarter. "What for?" I asked. He shrugged. I didn't take the quarter.

After that, we sat together every bus ride to school and back for a month. We looked sort of similar back then, the same height, though he was older and blond, and I have brown hair. We didn't have brothers or sisters. We were both quiet while other kids on the bus horsed around. We were comfortable with each other. Del would read his ratty, dog-eared paperbacks with stained covers. I read books from the library, or one of my dad's World War II histories.

I remember one time when Del was rummaging in his canvas sack for his latest paperback, piling odds and ends on the space between us—old tests and quizzes, pencil stubs, gum wrappers, a yellow metal box with "B.F. Gravely Superior Chewing Tobacco" embossed on the lid, and the school books for the day. On top of the pile I saw a crinkled-up math test, with 100% scrawled across the top in red, followed by an exclamation point. My God, I thought, this kid's smart. He reads books, and he's smart.

"That's cool," I said, pointing to the metal box. "You chew?"

Lots of kids chewed or smoked, especially the farm kids. But I'd never seen a tobacco tin before.

"Nah," he said. "Belonged to my grampa. It's. . . ." And he stopped mid-sentence. "It's a good luck charm."

"Can I see it?"

He looked me right in the eyes. "No," he said. "That's not a good idea. You wouldn't understand."

And I left it at that.

When we weren't reading on the bus, we talked about sports, or teachers, or TV shows. The only thing we didn't talk about was Del's family—never a word on them. We also didn't talk about what happened to Del the day he walked on the bus with a Band-Aid across his left cheek that wasn't big enough to cover even a quarter of the puffy bruise underneath.

"What happened to your face?" I asked.

"I fell."

"On your face? How'd that happen?"

Instead of answering, Del started methodically searching through his canvas sack, finally taking out a paperback titled *Sun Smasher*, with a cover showing a laser beam zapping an exploding sun. He started reading. I thought about asking my question again, but somehow knew I shouldn't. So I took out my book and read too, and we didn't talk during that ride. Every once in a while he'd press the Band-Aid, tenderly, with his fingertips.

One day Del didn't come out when the bus stopped at his house. Word went around that his mother had died of a blood cancer, and Del missed school for the rest of the week. The next time the bus picked him up, he sat alone near the front and stared out the window—the first time I could remember seeing him on the bus and not reading. I walked up to ask how he was doing, but he wouldn't answer. It was like he'd gone deaf. I felt hurt by that, then thought that if my mother had died, I might not talk to anyone for a while either. So I went back to my seat. I stared at the back of his blond head the whole ride, wondering what he could be thinking. After school that day, he didn't show up for the bus ride home.

The next morning, he again slumped into a seat by himself near the front.

"I heard about your mom," I said, settling beside him.

When he turned to face me, he had a black eye and puffy lip. Then he opened his mouth to show a missing front tooth.

"How'd that happen?"

"None of your fucking beeswax," he replied, as if he hadn't just deliberately showed me the missing tooth.

He turned back to the window.

After that day, Del forgot who I was. He pressed a button, and I got deleted from his memory. And also deleted from existence. He wouldn't say hi. He wouldn't see me. He'd walk past, or see through me. He started hanging out with the tough kids at our school, eventually becoming their leader. This is when he failed a grade. After turning sixteen he got a driver's license and stopped using the bus. I'd see him cruise into the school parking lot in the beat-up Pontiac Grand Prix inherited from his grandfather, with three or four guys piled in, and eventually Vera too.

———

The washing machine started up, and I heard Dad stomping upstairs. I plopped myself on the couch in the TV room to scan the comics. The shower rattled on, rattled off. Fifteen minutes later I heard Dad on the kitchen phone.

"That's right, Jack. ACT 236 New York. Blue. American. No, couldn't get the make. Would you check it out? No, that's all I got. Hang on." And I heard him shout, "Justin, remember anything else about that plate? I only saw ACT 236."

"Sorry," I shouted back. "Didn't see it."

"How about the make and model?"

"Nope. Drawing a blank." And in my head I told him exactly what I thought. Let it go! That's a snake's pit of trouble, so please let it go.

"Jack," Dad said, back on the phone. "Those kids could have killed us. High school, sixteen or seventeen. . . . Yeah, that's right. Not that you could prove it now. . . . All right. Give me a call when you get something, OK?"

Their conversation turned to how East Liberty was going to—you guessed it—"hell in a handbasket": juvenile delinquents, bankruptcies, drugs, burglaries, so on, so forth. How kids these days don't have stable families or safe places to go out to in the evenings. Stable families? I wanted to say. Like ours? And what's hell got to do with a handbasket? What's a handbasket got to do with kids taking drugs or tossing a super-size cup of piss? Sometimes it wasn't what Dad said but the way he said it that was so irritating I needed to answer, loudly, in my head: *Relax! Be like other dads. Kick back with a beer and some TV.* The truth was, if Dad popped a Miller Lite at a neighborhood barbecue in the summer, it was a big deal. People actually noticed. And forget about TV, unless it was news on public television, or a gloomy black and white movie set in Europe.

———

Dinner was pork chops, tater tots, broccoli. I could handle tater tots, but those over-cooked, dried-out chops and the soggy dark-green broccoli from a freezer packet made me queasy. While Dad talked, I cut everything into different-size pieces except the tater tots.

"You should have heard Jack Boland going on about East Liberty. Vandalism in Oak View cemetery, swastikas spray-painted on the synagogue, beer parties in Hopkins Park, pot smoking on school grounds. Even in the basement of Our Lady of Lourdes!

Even methamphetamine, can you believe it? Six months ago I thought that was something you took for the flu. Now it's a major industry in upstate New York. And last summer, that business at the Barkley farm. Who'd have guessed? What's going on?"

That "business at the Barkley farm" was the biggest thing to happen in East Liberty I could remember. Hank Barkley had been on a six-month drinking binge and not making mortgage payments. So the bank foreclosed, and his solution was to blow off his wife's head with a shotgun and then hang himself from a barn rafter. Problem solved. Problem just blown away. It was all we saw on the local news for a week. The only photograph they showed was Hank Barkley with his arm around his wife, both in their mid-twenties, as blissed-out as newlyweds could be in front of their ranch-style house—the same house where he shot off her head.

"So Mr. Boland doesn't know who was in the car?" I said.

"No, but he'll find out. Computer databases and all that."

"Do they have computers in the East Liberty station?"

"They must," Dad said. He wrinkled his brow. "Not that I've seen any."

"I'm sorry," I said, "but Mr. Boland looks like he types with two fingers. You know, needing five minutes to peck out his name, and spelling it wrong."

Dad laughed. "You're probably right. But Jack's a good cop. He cares about East Liberty. He knows more than most about how the tanked economy is destroying this community. The Blake farm's one of the few family farms left. No one can figure how Fulton Blake keeps going. Scrawny cows fenced in a dirt yard. Must be up to his eyebrows in debt. Looks terrible as well. Did you hear about his dog?"

"No."

"He kept a pit bull on a chain in the farmyard. Typical around East Liberty these days. The turned-over water dish. The empty food dish. No shelter from sun or rain. But the thing got loose, ran to the next farm, and broke the neck of every chicken in the chicken coop."

"What happened to it?"

"Blake's neighbor shot it dead, that's what happened." Dad shook his head and stabbed a tater tot.

"I'm done," I said. "I'll check out the TV."

"I'm not finished," Dad said.

"That's because you've been talking while I've been eating. See?" I showed my plate of cut up broccoli and meat.

"I'd rather not eat alone," Dad said. "We're still a family, you know."

He speared a chunk of pork. He chewed. Chewed harder. "What's your day like tomorrow?"

"A math quiz. In music we're doing Appalachian folk songs. In English it's *Macbeth*. In history it's World War II."

"World War II?" Dad said. "You're an expert."

"Playing games isn't the same as taking tests, Dad," I answered, though in fact I'd learned a lot about that war by playing board games and reading comics, novels, and history books.

"Where's Grandpa's medal anyway?" I asked. "The one you never let me touch."

Dad laughed. "I never let you touch it because everything you touched when you were a kid, you broke. Like your grandmother's Christmas music box with the blue dancing horses. Remember that?"

"Dancing horses? I don't remember dancing horses. And you can't break a medal."

"It wouldn't have been right for you to play with Grandpa's medal. That medal. . . ." He paused. "That's important to me."

"So where's it now?"

"Top drawer of my bedroom dresser. Want to see it?"

"No, that's OK." My goal was *less* conversation, not more.

"What history assignments are you getting about World War II?"

"Mr. Horn paired everyone up for presentations on the war."

"Who's your partner?"

"Jamie Peterson."

"Well, well." He smiled, and then he winked. He *winked*.

"Lovely girl," he said. "I met her in her dad's store. You got lucky."

Jamie and I were supposed to go over ideas for the presentation during lunch the next day. I couldn't imagine that lunch. Lovely? Lucky? Those words didn't get near what was happening. Jamie's family had money. She was smart and hot. Intimidating. Totally out of my league.

"And I knew her dad Hank Peterson in high school," Dad continued. "He and his cousin Fulton Blake were best friends then. He moved back here from Brooklyn to open that clothing store on Genesee Street, didn't he? It's great that a guy has the faith to come back and make a commitment to this community. Must be a hard slog selling high-end men's suits in this town. He's got to be a fantastic businessman. They say next year he'll be president of the Chamber of Commerce."

"Dad," I said, "I'm finished with dinner."

"Can you believe Hank Peterson and Fulton Blake were best friends in high school? Inseparable—you didn't see one without the other being somewhere nearby. Hard to imagine, isn't it, how things change?"

When I didn't answer, he ate a piece of broccoli, chewed, and then frowned.

"Speaking about families moving to East Liberty," he said, "you know Danh next door?"

"Of course I know Danh."

"Why don't you bike with him to school?"

"He's a year younger than me. I'm on the edge of being a geek. If I bike to school with him, I'll cross the line."

"It can't be easy for that family in this community," Dad said, "especially for the boy. We're too tied up in ourselves here. You should make Danh feel welcome. It's silly that you wait at the window until you see him leave."

How's he know that? I wondered. Just when Dad seems most out of it, he surprises me with what he sees.

"And there's worse things than being a geek. You could be a methamphetamine addict painting swastikas on a synagogue."

"All right," I groaned. "I'll bike to school with Danh. Can I go now?"

"Go. Go do whatever's so important. TV, right? Something extraordinarily important on TV. Go ahead. You have my permission. Go."

———

I was free.

I'd missed the first ten minutes of *American Dad*. On top of that, my stomach was gurgling from the tater tots. I was hungry but couldn't imagine eating anything from our fridge. I felt guilty. Dad's "go do whatever's so important" was typical Dad-speak, meaning, *sure, watch your meaningless TV junk while your poor father eats dinner alone. He doesn't have anyone to talk with except his only child, who'd rather stare at the idiot box than have a meaningful conversation.*

It's amazing what Dad can pack into four words. Or two. Or one, like *"Really?"* which in Dad-speak means, *I don't believe anything you just said.*

———

That night I kept waking from dreams when I'd be doing something normal, like mowing the lawn or drying dishes, and suddenly there'd be Del Blake's crazy grinning face with its missing tooth in the window of a passing car, or lit in a doorway by a spotlight, or alone at a table in the school cafeteria, or under water in a gigantic aquarium in our living room, murky green with algae, swarming with guppies dribbling bubbles from their mouths.

In one dream Tommy DeSantis's hand tossed a bucket of piss through the bedroom window, soaking me and the bed.

Dad's face popped in and out, his lips tight with anger.

I saw Mom's face once—sad, but more than sad, *sadly angry* would maybe describe it.

There was that other face, too. The baby face in the crib just a few steps from my bed. I was supposed to have my own room by Christmas of that year—a remodeled storage room. But after little Mike died, work just stopped so our shared room became my room again. His crib was handmade from cherry by some far back ancestor—old fashioned, scuffed, banged-up. My war-hero grandfather slept in it when he was a baby. My dad too. And me. And then little Mike, who didn't live long enough to say my name because there was a problem with his lungs. Dad says he didn't cry out. Didn't make a sound. But I'm not so sure.

When little Mike died, something in our family died with him, a thing none of us understands even now, though we know it's real. We all started moving more slowly and stiffly.

Here's the question I don't ask out loud but that I'm always asking myself in my head: What could I have done? Did everything have to happen the way it happened? Did little Mike have to die?

3

Monday

WHEN I WOKE THE NEXT MORNING, I felt afraid. The first thing in my mind was Del Blake. The second was that Dad had asked his cop friend Jack Boland to track down Del's license plate. If Del got into trouble, he'd take it out on me. That was a given of high school in East Liberty in general, and of Del in particular—the only thing you could count on besides homework every night and relationship dramas in the cafeteria was a bully's need for revenge. But there was something different about Del. He wasn't big, he wasn't stupid. He could have been a normal smart kid, like he seemed back when we rode the bus to school together. He could have continued being a bookworm like me. We might have continued being friends. I don't know why, but he got sidetracked from being normal, which made him much worse than your usual stupid bully. Del had become a species of his own, a minnow who discovers his true self is a shark. The worst bullies in school were scared of Del Blake.

Once Del was walking across the school parking lot by himself. A bunch of kids had a game of touch football going. Jason Feeley, the biggest kid in seventh grade, caught a pass and took off towards the goal, which was the curb at the end of the lot. But when he dodged right to avoid a kid coming after him, he smashed into Del, who skidded on the pavement for a dozen feet. Instead of seeing if Del was OK, Jason kept on running, shouting "touchdown" and dancing a stupid jig like a football player on TV. Then

21

some kids on the other team started shouting that Jason had run out of bounds. No one checked on Del, though we all saw him lying there. I should have gone to see if he was OK, but I didn't. I just couldn't. He lay still, not making a sound, then slowly got up. An arm from the elbow to the wrist was skinned and bleeding; his jeans had ripped at both knees. The strange thing was that he didn't react to what had happened. His face had flushed, but he didn't show he was hurt. He certainly didn't cry. He just limped off school grounds heading God knows where, without looking back. Jason and his friends started playing football again as if what happened to Del hadn't really happened.

But Del knew it happened and didn't forget. A week later we heard that Jason Feeley had fallen over a school railing, down a fifteen-foot drop, breaking both legs and fracturing his skull. No one could just fall over one of those waist-high railings. You had to be pushed. Or maybe, beaten up and pushed. Jason's story was that he'd been hanging out with Del and Tommy DeSantis, just horsing around when he accidentally tripped and fell. After he got out of the hospital and back to school, I never saw him anywhere near Del again. If Del was at one end of the playground, you'd see Jason at the other end. In the halls, he talked and walked just a beat slower than before what he called his "accident." By summer, Jason's dad had sold the family dairy farm, and they moved to Maryland. The story made an impression on me: that Del could cause such a thing to happen, that he'd bide his time to get it done, and there'd be no consequences. Parents, teachers—even the police—no one could get to Del Blake because he knew how to figure things out. For Del, high school was a war zone, and he was mobilized for combat. He was always thinking strategically. After Jason's "accident" Del seemed taller to me, and heavier, though he probably hadn't changed at all.

I calmed my nerves with the thought that Dad's friend Boland and the old dumb cop who worked with him, Daryl Monde, wouldn't be smart enough to track down license plates. Besides, with all the drug and crime problems popping up in East Liberty, there must be more important things to do than figure out which kid played which stupid prank on a country road. Dad, I hoped, would soon forget the whole business. He'd get wrapped up in more meaningless college politics involving a dozen names I can't remember—people who actually *enjoy* sitting around a table arguing about things that don't matter to anyone, not even themselves.

———

After I'd showered, dressed, stuffed my books and homework into my backpack, I peeked out the living room window toward Danh's house.

"Bye, Dad!" I yelled.

"Why don't you check if Danh wants to bike with you?"

"He already left."

I was waiting for Dad to shout back, *How would you know?* But he'd gotten preoccupied with searching for student papers he'd brought home. "OK," he called from the dining room—he always graded at the table. "I'll fix something for dinner." Mondays and Thursdays were Dad's long teaching days, with a two-hour morning class, an afternoon class from four to five, a three-hour evening class from seven to ten. So he always set out dinner for me. Mondays and Thursdays were also Mom's nights to call—when Dad was happy to be out of the house.

"Did you make your bed?" he shouted from the dining room.

"No time."

"Make it, or I'll make it."

Go ahead, I thought. What do I care?

"One more thing," he said, appearing in the front hall with the missing papers under an arm. "Is anything going on for you this Saturday?"

"No."

"I've been invited to dinner."

This was a surprise. Dad never went out to dinner. "Who invited you?"

"Reverend Haroldson."

An image from Sunday flashed through my mind: us in the line snaking out of church, Reverend Haroldson holding Dad's right hand in both of hers.

"I'll make you dinner before I leave," Dad said. "How about fish? They've got great fish at the P&C on a Friday."

"No," I said. "Remember that fish you cooked last week? Stunk so bad we had to throw it out, open the windows, and set up fans in the kitchen."

"That did stink," Dad said thoughtfully. "Cod past its date. I don't think that was me."

"It wasn't you, Dad. It was your cooking."

"Not my cooking, my shopping." He looked pleased to make that distinction.

"Just not fish, Dad," I said. "OK?"

———

I wheeled my bike from the garage—crammed with everything you can think of relating to cars except our actual car, a Honda Civic that Dad parked in the driveway.

"Just!" I heard. "Hey Justin! Wait up!"

Danh.

I was trapped. Any other day I would have taken off so fast Danh would never catch up. But I couldn't this morning. Not after Dad had made such a big deal about me avoiding him. Are Danh and I required to be friends because we're neighbors?

"We're going to school at the same time!" Danh shouted when he reached me.

"That's obvious, isn't it?" I said.

"Yeah. I guess." He looked confused.

Danh didn't talk during the bike ride to school like I thought he would. The only time he said anything was when he saw a stray cat on the corner of McDowell and Bishop, carrying something in its mouth to the lopsided porch of the old Jordan house. Ever since Mr. Jordan died the house had been empty, with broken front windows, peeling paint, a For Sale sign in the overgrown front yard. The Jordan house was definitely *not* a McMansion. But it had one surprising feature, an elaborate bird house for purple martins with a dozen round entrances, lots of little roofs, and a couple of patios—a bird mansion set on a pole anchored in concrete that my dad remembers from when he was a kid. But of course nothing was living there, since martins would have migrated south.

"Look!" Danh shouted. "That cat's got something, a mouse I think. Now it's under the porch." Danh was fixated. "Now it's out again."

"Who cares?" I said. "It's a cat."

But when Danh stopped biking to watch it run across the driveway and dive into a hedge, I stopped too. When it reappeared with something else in its mouth, we saw that the something else was a kitten. We laid our bikes down, snuck up, and peeked through the slats under the porch. Though it was dark in there, we could make out the cat curled in a depression in the ground. A mother with four nursing kittens. You'd think staring at kittens would be for little kids but in fact it was amazing how they squirmed their tiny bodies, how the mother lay on her side and let them suck so hard it had to hurt.

Monday morning, and even the teachers were sleepwalking. In social studies Mr. Daniels droned on about the Great

Depression and how that related to the upstate farm economy. By the end, he'd spread the Great Depression all over the room. In gym we played basketball, which the coach thought I should be good at since I'm tall and skinny. But my hands and legs don't like to cooperate. So it was basically dribble up the court, shoot and miss, wait your turn, dribble down, shoot and miss, wait your turn, then do the whole meaningless exercise again . . . proving and reproving how incapable you are of making the shot.

And being skinny wasn't exactly great for football, the main sport at East Liberty High, followed by basketball, followed by wrestling, followed by . . . followed by nothing. That was it. Dad would always tell me: You're rail thin! A beanpole! Eat! I might have bulked up if Dad could cook; or if Saturday's leftover Domino's pizza didn't do an encore on Sunday, then sneak in next to boiled peas on Monday, and take a final bow on Tuesday when every drop of moisture had evaporated from it. Was I a garbage disposal Dad could scrape leftovers into? With my fork I stabbed that slice of cardboard topped with shriveled pepperoni, held it up, and walked it to the garbage. I thought Dad might get angry, but he laughed.

"You're right," he said. "Put the thing out of its misery."

———

In the cafeteria I couldn't see Jamie. The freshmen were clumped as usual near the door, where they could most easily escape harassment. Basketball players always clustered in the middle. Del Blake and his criminal friends, including Tommy and Will, sat at a far right corner table, on the edge of everything.

Normally I'd eat lunch with Rusty Taylor and Fred Gardiner, friends I also hung out with on weekends. I wasn't what you'd call popular—not like Marty Tower, who had friends at every table: he could even talk with Tommy and Will, though not with Del. I wasn't invited to join any of the fraternities that had started up at school, where kids would buy the same style jackets embroidered with their names and hang out together, believing that wearing the same jacket made them friends for life. Not that I wanted to join. Growing up, my best friend was a neighborhood kid, Richie Ryan, whose birthday was two days after mine. We spent every weekend at one or another's house. We both liked history and read the same comic books. It was Richie who really got me into World War II. We'd spend hours playing with these plastic army soldiers he collected, half of them green and half blue, some with rifles, some with bazookas, all as tall as our little fingers. We'd spend more hours playing *Axis and Allies*, a board game that belonged to Richie's older brother. And we'd watch war movies whenever we could. One time Richie's dad found us in the TV room with our army guys set up over the floor, and on all the tables, chairs, shelves, books. We were on our hands and knees with chins on the carpet because we needed a soldier's eye view of the battle.

"What's going on?" he asked Richie. "Did you lose something?"

"Dad," Richie said, as if he were talking to a child, "it's the battle for Stalingrad. Can't you see the house-to-house combat? The Germans under Paulus and the Russians under Zhukov. And the Germans are gonna lose again." Mr. Ryan just shook his head.

Why was I so into it? Maybe it had to do with how my parents were always dragging me around—to the kitchens of boring neighbors for a chat, to grocery stores and pharmacies. And if I wasn't being dragged around, I was forced to sit still—for homework, church services, or "family conferences" when I was given a list of things I could do better, like picking up my room or making my bed. In a war game Richie and I did the dragging. We were Rommel or Patton or Zhukov. We figured out the grand strategies.

I think there's another reason I'd gotten so interested: my grandfather. He was a real hero in that war, awarded the Medal of Honor by the president of the United States. It wasn't so much that I thought about him while I played war games. It was more like I felt him inside me. He was a part of me then, strong and focused and courageous, though I only knew him from photographs and my dad's stories.

But the Ryans moved out of East Liberty to Charlotte, North Carolina, when Richie's dad got laid off from Marietta. And of course Richie took his soldiers with him. We sent e-mails back and forth for a while, talked by phone a little, hatched plans to visit each other, but then just drifted apart, the way kids do, without realizing it's happening until it's happened.

It was after Richie moved from East Liberty that I started hanging out with Rusty and Fred. On a Saturday night we three sometimes caught a movie at the mall if one of our parents had a reason to go shopping. We sat together at school sports events and assemblies, a little row of three on a bleacher, with me in the middle. They came to my house some nights to watch TV, and I went to theirs. But we didn't have that much in common. I liked to read, Rusty liked baseball (watching, not playing), and Fred's favorite thing was model airplanes, which he put together with his dad every Sunday afternoon. About twenty of them plastered with decals hung in formation from his bedroom ceiling from almost invisible threads. What we most had in common was that we didn't fit into any neat slot: we didn't play sports, or do theater or music; we didn't fail grades but didn't get straight "A"s. We were sort of just ourselves. And then there was Rusty's bright red hair, Fred's leg brace, and my . . . whatever it was about me that didn't fit.

I got to know Rusty because we rode the same bus home, with Rusty getting off around ten minutes before me. We started talking one day about the Yankees and the World Series, and took off from there. How we then got to be friends with Fred involved

Del Blake. Rusty and I had decided to go to a school dance at the end of term. I didn't like dances because they were mostly about watching other people having fun, or pretending to have fun, but Rusty was hot to go and wanted company. He actually planned to ask girls to dance.

It was in the school gym, of course, with every bank of lights on full blast, the bleachers pushed back against the walls, and a local band set up on a platform. Couples were making out in corners where the lights didn't reach. Teacher and parent chaperones walked a loop around and around the dance perimeter looking for . . . God knows what they were looking for. They walked with eyes glazed over. If they stuck out their arms like zombies in old movies you wouldn't be surprised. The dance floor was a square marked off by white plastic cones, which the chaperones were supposed to keep clear of non-dancing kids. The band played covers of songs I didn't recognize. Or maybe I would have recognized if the band could play better: it was all bass guitar and thumping drums.

Rusty and I were just looking around the gym at everyone we didn't know or couldn't talk to when I saw Fred, standing by himself at the edge of the dance floor occupied by a half dozen couples. He was hunched to one side because of his brace, which clamped onto a black boot on his left foot. I knew who Fred was, and would say hi if I saw him in school or around town. His family had moved to East Liberty so his dad could work for Marietta. Basically his dad's job was to "downsize" the company, as Fred put it—so his family wasn't the most popular in town. In fact it was Fred's dad who told Richie's dad that he no longer had a job.

The band finished their song with a shrieking guitar crescendo, and a few whacks on a drum. About three kids clapped. Then the band started up again.

"Wanna to ask some girls to dance?" Rusty said.

"I don't dance," I said.

"It's a slow song. You just find a girl. You put your arms around each other, and you walk, or shuffle-walk, back and forth. Kind of like. . . ." He paused. "Kind of like vacuuming."

"So you've done it before?" I said.

"Not exactly."

"What exactly does 'not exactly' mean? You've either done it or you haven't."

"Well," he said, "I practice. You know, on my own."

I had a vision of Rusty in his living room, arms around a girl made of air, shuffling his gangly legs across the carpet to slow music on his dad's old stereo. Kind of like vacuuming, I guess. He's smiling. His eyes are closed. He's having a good time.

"Go ahead without me," I told him, adding "good luck" as he walked away. And I thought about how over the time I'd known him, Rusty didn't just get interested in girls. He'd gotten *really* interested. The only thing more important was baseball. The problem, of course, was getting *them* interested in *him*.

Beyond Fred at the other end of the gym I saw Del and Tommy, their backs against a stack of bleachers, not talking, just staring at the crowd. Even when Del is quiet and not moving, you can't help but notice him. He's like that one misspelled word in a sentence. When Will Hayes strode through the main door to the gym, I knew it was Will that Del and Tommy were looking for. A supposedly coordinated football player, Will was actually a huge klutz. If there was a crash of glass and plates on the cafeteria floor, it was Will you'd see standing nearby with an empty tray and shit-eating grin. He was a bulldozer—and bulldozers do one of two things: go forward, or in reverse. If it was really important, maybe a lurch left or right. Will was in forward mode. He bulldozed into the gym, swinging his arms like a Yeti I once saw on TV, and stopped a dozen feet in front of Fred. He then caught sight of Del, and started bulldozing through the couples on the dance floor. But when one of the zombie chaperones came to consciousness and forced him back, he picked up speed along the perimeter, moving into high gear but so oblivious that he slammed into Fred, who went sprawling across the floor over to where I stood.

"You idiot!" Will shouted at Fred. "What's the matter with you? What the hell's your deal?"

Then Will saw Fred's brace. "You're a cripple," he sneered. "What are you doing at a dance? You gonna hop around like some . . . like some hopping . . . rabbit?"

Fred stared up at Will. He gripped his brace with both hands, as if his leg hurt. I offered Fred a hand but he wouldn't take it, and struggled to his feet on his own.

Trying to help was a mistake, because that put Will's attention on me.

"You his friend?" he said, more an accusation than a question.

"No," I said. "Not really."

"Well, you're in the wrong place. You don't belong here. The both of you. You're aliens."

"Anyone can be here," I said. "We've got the same rights as you."

Those didn't seem like my words but words my dad would want me to say. I was suddenly so nervous that I curled my lower lip between my teeth and bit down. Maybe I did that to stop talking, because saying anything to Will Hayes would likely earn a beating. And what I'd just said wasn't even true. Will was at the dance because he really did belong. The gym was *his* place; for him the dance was familiar and welcoming. People were looking for him, even if those people were psychopaths like Del Blake and Tommy DeSantis. Fred, though, was probably here because his mother made him go, or because he thought other kids he knew would be here, or because he'd decided to take a risk. And I was here . . . I don't know why. Because of Rusty, I guess. I really had no right to be in the gym. I scanned around for a chaperone, but they'd all disappeared.

I wiped my lip with my hand, and was surprised by a smear of blood across my thumb. A metallic taste spread through my mouth. For some reason my eyes drifted over to Del, who was staring at me—no expression on his face, just these steady, unblinking eyes.

"OK, big mouth," Will said, stepping close to me. I winced from the out rush of beer breath.

He pointed to the floor, drawing a line with his finger. "Put some money where that big mouth is. Cross that line. I dare you. Cross it and I'll knock out every tooth you own. And that's for starters."

Of course there wasn't a line, just a vague place where his finger might have pointed. How would he know if I stepped over or not? It didn't matter. Moving an inch anywhere would earn a beating. That was the whole point. To find a reason to start a fight.

"Move," he said. "Don't be a sap."

Of course I didn't. I'd become a statue.

"Will!" a voice called out. It was Del shouting from across the gym. He was standing up now, his hands cupped around his mouth. Will turned to face him.

"Get over here! Now!" Del jerked his head to the left, indicating impatience. "Now!"

Will turned to me and Fred, standing side by side. "You're both . . ." he began, searching for words, "you're both . . . ," but he couldn't find words to end the sentence. He squinted at the ceiling, as if words might be available up there. "You're both . . . big mouth cripples," he said finally, relying on what had worked before. "All three of you," he added, including Rusty, who'd just joined us. "You're three hopping rabbit cripples." Satisfied he'd made his point, Will hauled himself across the empty dance floor to join Del and Tommy.

I wondered, did Del decide to save me? Or was he just impatient to get Will moving?

"Thanks," Fred said when Will was far away.

"For what?" I asked.

He shrugged. "I don't know. For being . . . for being a cripple." Fred tended to say things bluntly. "And a hopping rabbit. And a big mouth. And an alien. Thanks for being an alien."

"You're welcome," I said, "I guess."

"What just happened?" Rusty asked.

"Will Hayes felt like beating someone up," I said. "And we qualified as someone. But we got away with no bones broken and no loss of blood."

"Your lip is bleeding," Fred said. He laughed a little. "It's gross. And he didn't even hit you."

"I know," I said, and wiped again with my hand. "I did it to myself."

"Have a good dance?" I asked Rusty.

He shook his head sheepishly. "I asked, like, ten girls, and they all said no."

"Ten?" I said. "I'd rather get beaten up by Will Hayes than ask ten girls to dance."

"Hey," Rusty said, suddenly distracted. "Free popcorn and soda over there." He pointed to a table where a sour-looking Mr. Horn sat surrounded by little paper bags of popcorn and huge bottles of soda. That's something I liked about Rusty. He wasn't much bothered when things didn't go his way. After the ninth girl, he'd still forge ahead and ask the tenth. And if that didn't work, he'd find something to eat. So the three of us walked to the popcorn table. I got in line behind Rusty and Fred, though I couldn't imagine putting anything into a stomach tied up in knots.

"Enjoying yourself?" Horn asked, handing me a crumpled bag of popcorn. He was older than my dad, sixty at least.

"Yeah," I said. "It's . . . fun."

Mr. Horn smiled and shook his head.

"I've been there," he said. "I've skipped the light fandango just like you. Here," he held out a napkin. "Do you know your lip is bleeding?"

The band announced that they'd now play the final song of the night—and just when I thought that all drama possible in an East Liberty high school dance had played out, I saw a crazy thing. Donny Schill and three of his lowlife friends were heading for the popcorn table. Donny stopped, touched the cheek with the patch of bad acne, then started waving his arms at his friends and shouting—but his voice was so high and screechy I could only understand the word "popcorn." Then he shut up in mid-sentence, dropped his arms, hunched his shoulders, and fell backwards like a sawed-through tree. I actually heard his head smack the floor just before the band started playing. Even though his head was still, his arms and legs flailed and thrashed on their own, as if they didn't belong to him. His eyes rolled up into his head, so all you could see were the spooky whites. His friends stared at him for a few seconds—it seemed like everything in the gym was still except Donny's arms and legs. Then they bolted towards the front door—not, it turns out, the best friends in the world. Mr. Horn shoved aside the popcorn table in a rush to get to Donny. Then other kids started crowding around while Horn shouted for them to "keep back!" and "give him room to breathe!"

"Epilepsy" someone behind me said. But another voice answered, "No way. Donny Schill's a tweaker. He's finally fried his brain."

———

My dad had made me a bag lunch. But I thought that when Jamie showed up, she might think it was lame for me to eat a lunch my dad made, so I dropped it in the trash. I could buy a $2.50 hot lunch because I had five dollars in my wallet. The hot lunch turned out to be sloppy joe—a hamburger bun with runny reddish junk piled on, mushy green beans on the side whether you wanted them or not. I got a glass of milk. Then I wished I hadn't thrown away Dad's lunch.

I found an empty table where I could save a chair for Jamie, so the two of us could talk about the presentation. Then Danh walked in with a bag lunch and a can of Sprite. I kept my eyes on my food, but of course he saw me and walked over.

"Hey, Just."

"Oh, hi, Danh."

He stood there. "Can I sit with you?"

"I'm meeting Jamie Peterson. About our presentation."

Danh stared at the seat next to me as if Jamie might be invisible.

"She'll be here any minute," I said.

"Can I sit until she comes?"

"Sure."

"Is this seat OK?"

"Sit where you want. There aren't rules about where you sit," which of course wasn't true. There were plenty of rules—hard and fast rules—just not written down.

As soon as he sat across from me and took a sandwich from his lunch bag, Jamie arrived, a big smile on her face. She looked fantastic in a red top, short blue jean skirt with red leggings, blonde hair pulled into a ponytail, a diamond stud in each pierced ear, everything perfect. Though I must have seen her a thousand times since she'd moved to East Liberty my freshman year, I'd never been this close before. She smelled great. I noticed a half-moon scar above her left eyebrow and wondered if she noticed me noticing the scar. She was my age, but seemed older. That's usually the case with girls my age, but even more with Jamie. When she smiled, you paid attention.

"Sorry I'm late." She glanced at Danh. "Can I join you?"

I couldn't answer.

"Maybe it's not a good time?"

"It's fine," I said. "We're not doing anything."

"We're not doing anything," Danh said.

Jesus Christ, I thought. He's become an echo. Now every stupid thing I say is going to be said twice so Jamie will be sure not to miss it.

Jamie set her tray down and removed a sandwich from her backpack. A wrap—something her mother would have bought instead of made. I was suddenly aware of a grease spot from Dad's cooked breakfast on the pocket of my wrinkled blue shirt. When did that happen? I just glanced down, and it was all I could see, like a full moon in the dead of night.

"Can I stay?" Danh said.

"Of course," Jamie said. "We'd like you to stay."

"Of course you can," I said, realizing that I'd now become Jamie's echo.

"You're Danh, right?" She pronounced "Danh" the way our history teacher Mr. Horn said it when calling roll—"Yen"—the Vietnamese way.

He nodded.

"Does 'Danh' have a meaning in Vietnamese?"

He checked around himself quickly, as if worried someone might overhear, then said, "It means 'famous.' That's what my dad told me."

I looked at Jamie, but there wasn't a flicker of a smile, though most kids would have laughed out loud at the idea of such a name for Danh, the least famous kid in school.

"And we're in history together."

He nodded again.

"Did you skip a grade?" she asked. "I hope you don't mind me asking."

"Yeah, a few years ago."

"Well, in history you ask great questions," she said, and he smiled this really big smile.

"Do you like your name pronounced the American way or the Vietnamese way?"

Danh pursed his lips, thinking hard. "I don't care," he said. "Either is good. Most kids just call me Dan."

"OK," she said. "Dan." She turned to me. "Any ideas about our presentation? What're you thinking about?"

I was going to make something up on the spot, when I saw Del Blake and Tommy DeSantis get up from their table and start walking towards our table, with Vera Knight a few steps behind. Del was shorter than Tommy but always seemed bigger—like a scary optical illusion. His dirty blond hair was buzz cut to his scalp. Besides missing a front tooth, the thing about Del that most got your attention were his intense blue eyes, which looked not just at you, but into you, or through you.

I was holding my breath until he walked by on his way to whatever trouble he was making somewhere else because, after all, I didn't exist. But he didn't walk by. He stopped when he reached our table.

"Hey, cousin," Del said to Jamie.

"Hi, Del."

He turned to me. For some reason, I existed.

"I saw you on Sunday"—the first words he'd said to me in four years. "You and your dad."

"Yeah?" I said.

"You guys have a good walk?"

"Yeah."

"No bird shit drop out of the sky?"

"No."

"You sure? Thought I saw some on your dad's sweater."

Tommy, who'd been quiet up to now, burst into laughter.

"No."

"Nothing wet?"

"No."

"Well, that's good. That's real good. Piss can rain down from a clear sky. Bad things can happen on a country walk. Believe me, I should know. A good guy gets stabbed in the heart for no reason. Know what I mean?"

I nodded. My face suddenly felt really hot.

"Yeah," he said to no one in particular. "That's the way it is."

He turned to Danh. "What the hell are you?"

Danh squinted up at him, trying to figure out what answer would be most innocuous.

"My name's Danh," he said, pronouncing his name the American way.

"How d'you spell that?"

Danh spelled his name.

"Jesus." Del grinned broadly. "Just like 'Dan' except with a stupid extra letter. Don't your parents know how to spell?"

Tommy let out a loud guffaw. I glanced at Vera, who was staring at me with unblinking brown eyes. Her hands—which must have been scabbed up from her fall on my street—were balled into fists.

"Wow!" Jamie said to Del, her voice clear and even, sort of piercing. "That's original. And so very funny. I'll have to remember that one. I'll bet no one's *ever* thought of making fun of how Vietnamese people spell their names. You're a real genius. I think you're actually *accelerated*."

"What'd you say?" The way Del snarled out the words would have sent most kids running. But Jamie wouldn't be bullied.

"I said, that's such an original thing to say, you know, so funny, something I never could have thought up in a million, billion years." She smiled brightly. "You are *so* smart."

Del either couldn't think of anything scary to say, or realized he wouldn't win a battle of words with Jamie. Tommy nervously shifted his gaze from Del to Jamie and back. Vera kept creepily staring at me.

"I'll see you later," Del said, pointing a finger at my head, his thumb cocked. "And you too," he said to Danh. "You know, my Grampa Herd killed a bunch of you in Vietnam. Guess he had a helluva good time. Gooks in a barrel."

"See you Jamie," Tommy said, but she ignored him. "And you too, Danny," he added. And the three of them headed to the door, Vera keeping a few steps behind.

"What was that about?" Jamie asked when they'd gone. She turned to me. "And why was that girl staring at you? She follows Del like she's his indentured servant."

"I have no idea why they came over," I said. "Anyways, shouldn't we figure out our presentation?"

"Are you sure I can stay?" Danh asked.

"You can stay," I said. And I added, "I want you to stay."

"OK," Jamie said. "Forget those creeps. What Del said to Danh was disgusting. It just shows how pathetic he is, him and his cretin friends. Let's start our work. What are you interested in doing for our presentation?" She bit into her sandwich.

I said the first thing that came into my head.

"My grandfather got a Medal of Honor during World War II."

"Really?" Jamie said. "Isn't that a big deal?"

"I guess."

"What'd he do?"

"Dragged wounded soldiers off a hill during the Battle of the Bulge."

"He saved their lives?

"He got them down to a medic while that hill was being shelled. Then he went back up one last time and didn't come

down. When soldiers found him, they thought he was dead—
there was a dead guy in his arms—but he made some kind of
noise and they carried him down."

"Did he live?"

"Yeah, but he died later, in Berlin."

I'd gotten the story from my dad, who'd heard it from Grandpa's friend Ollie Johnston, a GI who was there. After the war,
Grandpa was stationed in Berlin, his back against a wall, eating
a K-ration, when a sniper put a bullet through his heart. Ollie
had been leaning against that same wall, a couple of feet from
Grandpa. That's all that happened. Eating food from a can one
minute, the next minute, dead.

"Why don't we use your grandfather's war experience in our
presentation?" Jamie said. "We'll give the history of the Medal
of Honor, who got one and why. And you could talk about your
grandfather. Horn would love it. He's a vet, right?"

"Vietnam vet," I said, then swallowed hard, wondering if that
would bother Danh. "But Horn won't talk about it."

"Let's do this." Jamie took another bite of her wrap then
fetched a pad and pen from her backpack. "Horn says we can't
just use the web. We've got to include books in our research."

"My dad's got a ton of World War II books," I said. "And I can
do web research and use the school library." What I didn't say was
that I'd been a World War II geek since the moment I first saw a
toy soldier.

"OK," Jamie said. "You dig into the history. I'll put together
profiles of Medal of Honor soldiers. We'll give the big picture but
you'll tell your grandfather's story to make it real, OK?"

"OK."

"Let's meet for lunch tomorrow," Jamie said. "Bring the medal
and your notes, and we'll get organized. Sound good?"

"Sounds good." Now I was doing that echo thing again.

"Can I come too?" Danh coughed into his hand. "Even if I'm not part of your actual group?"

"Of course," Jamie said.

"Sure," I said. I almost said *of course* but stopped myself. "Why not?"

After seeing that Jamie and Danh had finished their sandwiches, I picked up my sloppy joe, but set it back down. Besides being sloppy, it didn't smell good.

"How's your lunch?" Danh asked.

"Great," I said.

"You haven't eaten much," Jamie said.

"I'm full from breakfast."

Jamie stood and lifted her tray. "Got to go. I'm meeting with Marty for a biology project. Busy day! See you guys later."

After she was out the door and down the hall, Danh started in.

"She's amazing. She's the prettiest, smartest, prettiest girl in school. And she's nice. And she's smart."

"You already said she's smart."

"She knows how to handle Del Blake, doesn't she? She's not afraid at all. She shut him right up. What would have happened if she wasn't here?"

"I don't know," I said. "I don't want to think about that."

"How is it possible that she's Del's cousin?"

"It's definitely weird they're cousins," I said. "My dad says Del's dad and Jamie's were best friends in high school."

"But not now?"

"I guess not."

"Jesus. I can't believe Del Blake actually walked up to our table and didn't . . . you know, hurt one of us."

"Yeah," I said, swallowing hard.

"Who's Marty, anyway?" Danh said next.

"Marty?"

"The guy Jamie's working with on her biology project."

"Marty Tower, our class vice-president. He's on the football team."

Can Danh be so completely out of it, I thought, that he doesn't even know Marty Tower?

4

Monday

MR. HORN'S HISTORY CLASS was my last of the day, and the only one that Jamie, me, Danh, Del, and Tommy took together. Jamie sat ahead of me, two rows to my right; Del in the far left row; Danh was opposite on my right; Tommy at the far left in the back. Donny Schill was so slumped he could have been made of rubber, which is pretty much how he'd been since that seizure—or whatever it was—at the dance. We found out that he went to the emergency room that night. Then his dad brought him home and the next day he was back at school. Donny wouldn't talk about what had happened—it was as if nothing had happened, except that after the dance he went from being the kid who'd never shut up to the kid made of rubber, who couldn't talk.

On this day Mark Ransom was supposed to present on the Battle of El Alamein in North Africa. Our dentist's son, Mark had the bad luck of getting paired with Del Blake. As Mr. Horn called roll, I thought back to the last presentation I'd heard Del give, in Mrs. McShane's English class. We were studying *The Autobiography of Benjamin Franklin*—all about how great Franklin thought he was—and our assignment was to say something about our family history, using photographs. Most kids brought in a snapshot and said something lame like, "This is me eating a hot dog in Old Forge last summer." Or "This is me in my backyard in front of a sprinkler."

When Mrs. McShane called on Del, he shrugged and turned to the window. "Show and tell is for babies."

"All right, Del," Mrs. McShane said, her smile shrinking. "Just say a few words about your grandparents. That'll be sufficient. How about your father's father? Just a few words."

"He's dead."

"I'm sorry to hear that." The smile shrunk to nothing. "How about your mother's father?"

"Dead."

"Really?"

"Yup. My mother's dead too."

"I'm so sorry, Del."

"Actually, Grandpa Herd isn't dead." He turned to face Mrs. McShane, an odd twist to his lips—the creepy imitation of a smile. "We just tell people he's dead. He's in Attica for what he did to Gramma Herd."

Mrs. McShane stared at him for a few seconds. She definitely didn't want to pursue *that* subject. "Why don't you tell us what your father does for a living?"

"A broke dairy farmer. He's on food stamps. The farming thing is a joke."

Del spoke as if he was talking about people related to someone else.

"I think we'll move on," Mrs. McShane said.

All color had drained from her face. I knew she was considering her options. She couldn't send Del to the principal's office because while his attitude was disrespectful, he'd answered her questions and told the truth. Del's dad really *was* a broke dairy farmer. He hadn't done any real farming for years. He was on food stamps. And although Mrs. McShane didn't know it, because she'd only been at the school for two years, all the kids knew that Del's grandfather, Frank Herd, had fought in Vietnam, and one day, a couple years after he was home from the war, went berserk and beat Del's grandmother to death with a ball peen hammer, then dressed up in his old army fatigues and stabbed her dead body with his army knife like she was some kind of enemy. The rumor was he couldn't button the army shirt over his huge belly, so it was only buttoned near his neck. Then he called the police and sat down in front of the TV, watching baseball until they arrived. That's what got him a life sentence in the State Penitentiary. Del didn't say those things about his family to get sympathy. He said them because they were true.

Mark and Del's presentation was OK. They'd scripted a conversation between the English General Montgomery and the German Field Marshal Rommel. Del read the Montgomery part in a bored monotone, but Mark made up for it with a heavy German accent for Rommel. He was short and fat, and made his face stern. His act got a few girls giggling but definitely kept our attention. He worked in interesting details, like how Rommel was sick at a sanatorium in Germany when Hitler made him go to North Africa to command the German forces. Whenever Mark gave a little speech as Rommel, Del stared out the window, as if it had nothing to do with him.

"I'm impressed," Mr. Horn said, "that you two pulled this off."

Del started towards his seat.

"Wait. We're not done. Anyone have a question?"

No hands went up.

"This won't do," Mr. Horn said. "I need a question."

Danh raised his hand. "What happened to the cats? What did the cats do when the bombs were blasting?"

And Jamie thinks you ask interesting questions? I thought. Cats? Jesus!

"I have no idea," Mark said, shaking his head. "Cats never entered my mind."

"OK," Mr. Horn said. "Here's a question for Del. Cooperation is part of the assignment, so you two had to split the research and the writing fifty-fifty."

"I know," Del said.

"Of course you know," Mr. Horn said, "because you're a cooperative fellow, aren't you?"

"You bet," Del said.

"My question is about research. You can't just rely on the web. What are your book sources?"

Del shuffled his papers, then started reading.

"I researched at the town library and on the internet. My main book sources were *Alamein* by Jon Latimer and *War in the Desert* by James Lucas." He read in the same monotone used for the presentation.

Mr. Horn frowned. "Mark," he said, "did you write that for Del?"

"We split everything fifty-fifty," Mark said.

"Are you telling the truth? This is serious. I'm not fooling around."

Mark nodded. "Yes. Fifty-fifty." He glanced at Del, as if awaiting orders.

"Let me see your notes, Del."

Del's notes must have been in his handwriting because Mr. Horn seemed disappointed.

Jesus, I said to myself, Del thought of everything. He figures out every detail, and never gets caught.

———

The next presentation was Danh and Donny Schill on the Holocaust and Auschwitz. Danh mostly gave facts and figures: when Auschwitz was built, how many people died there, how they'd been tricked into the gas chambers—he really knew his stuff. Donny, though, pronounced "genocide" with a hard "g" and read each word as if it had no connection to the one he'd just said or the one he was about to say. He couldn't get through "extermination," so after three tries skipped to the next sentence. Maybe his brain really had gotten fried. As he talked, the acne cluster on his cheek got more and more inflamed. Mr. Horn stared intently at him the whole time. When he finished, I thought Horn would get on Donny's case like he had with Del. But he told Donny and Danh to sit down.

Mr. Horn stood and put his hands on his desk, as if to steady himself. "None of you could bear to hear the full story of Auschwitz," he said. "It can't be taught. It can hardly be talked about, at least not by me. It's just too horrific."

———

I walked with Danh out of history class and we ended up biking back home together.

"How come your mom doesn't live with you?" Danh asked when we'd reached my house. He said this as if we were in the middle of a conversation.

"Is that your business?" I said.

"I guess not."

"We're all fine," I said, though Danh hadn't asked how we were.

"Does your dad cook your dinner?"

"He'll leave something. He's working tonight."

"What will he leave?"

"A can of beef stew, or something."

"Sounds scary," Danh said, "especially the 'or something' part."

That was the first funny thing I could remember Danh saying.

"Yes," I said, "the 'or somethings' are scary."

"Why don't you come to my house for dinner?"

"No thanks," I said. "Got to work on my presentation."

"We eat at five-thirty. There's plenty of time for homework after dinner."

I thought about this. I really didn't want to eat whatever can of stuff Dad had left on the stove. And Danh, it turns out, was OK. He was the only kid who'd ever asked me about my mom. Not even Fred or Rusty broached that subject. It's true that I didn't answer Danh's question and got angry when he asked, but at least he asked.

"OK," I said. "I need to stop home first."

We stood there for a few seconds, watching squirrels chase each other in circles on the grass.

"See you soon," I said, and wheeled my bike into the garage.

In the kitchen I found a can of spaghetti with tomato sauce next to a can opener. A can of spaghetti tastes exactly like, well, a can of spaghetti. I put it in the cupboard and the opener in a drawer, and my eyes settled on the wall phone. Mom would call this evening. She phoned every Monday and Thursday at seven o'clock, nights when Dad would be teaching. I felt glad that I had some place to be until then.

———

I'd only been in Danh's house once, a week after his family had moved in, when Mom baked an apple pie and the three of us walked over to welcome them to the neighborhood. We sat around their kitchen table, and they served coffee to Mom and Dad, a Coke for me, and we all had a slice of pie. I didn't say much. I mostly stared at Danh's parents: I'd never seen Vietnamese people close-up. While Mr. Phan had an accent, Mrs. Phan sounded as American as Mom. And the more I stared, the more beautiful she seemed, with long black hair, perfect skin, dressed in jeans and a purple shirt, and this really big, friendly smile. Every once in a while she'd ask me a question:

"What subjects do you like at school?"

"History, sometimes English."

"Do you play any sport?"

"Not unless I have to, and I have to almost every day," an answer that made her laugh.

"Do you like to read?"

"Yes, I do," I said. "I like it a lot." And it occurred to me that no adult had ever asked if I liked to read.

Mr. Phan was taller than I thought the Vietnamese were supposed to be. He and Mrs. Phan took turns calling for Danh to come down, but he stayed in his room the whole time. The next week he showed up at school looking completely terrified. I'd say "hi" if I ran into him around the neighborhood or in school, but that was it.

———

Danh opened the door a few seconds after I knocked.

"Hey," he said, "you're here." I had the impression he'd been standing at the door waiting. Then his mother and a yapping dog appeared.

"Binh!" she shouted, and the dog shut up and sat down.

"This is Justin," Danh said.

"I remember," she said. "Thank you for joining us. Please come in." This time she was wearing blue jeans and a red blouse.

"Can you boys entertain yourselves? Come down in a half hour, OK?"

Danh's bedroom was large and incredibly neat. Even his bed was made. On a table in one corner was a fancy marble chess set.

"Where'd you get this?" I asked.

"It's Dad's. We play for a half hour every night before bed." A worried look came over his face. "I could have beat him last week."

"Yeah?"

"I saw checkmate in six moves."

"What happened?"

"I made a wrong move."

"That's OK," I said. "I mean, he's older. He's your father."

"No," Danh said. "I made a wrong move on purpose. I didn't want to win. Then he checkmated me in four."

"You must be pretty good," I said. "I wish I was that good at something."

"I'm OK. How about cards? What to play something? Pitch?"

We played a few hands of Pitch, all of which I won, and I asked where he'd lived before they moved to East Liberty.

"Santa Clara. Before that, Providence. Before that, Atlanta. Dad doesn't like staying any place more than two years."

"Is that because there aren't any"—I started to say *of your people* but caught myself—"any Vietnamese in those cities?"

"There's plenty. Dad doesn't want to be around Vietnamese people."

"But you're Vietnamese."

"I was born in this country," Danh said. "Mom too. It's only Dad who lived in Vietnam when he was little. Dad says it's complicated, who left Vietnam when and why and how. Who stayed behind. He says people have strong feelings about it. Anyway, Dad's American now."

"Do you like moving around?"

"I like being in one place. The same place. Dad writes computer software for games so we pretty much can live wherever he wants. Ever hear of 'Extreme Quest'?"

"I think so," I said.

"He invented that game."

"If you can live anywhere, why East Liberty?"

Danh shrugged. "Dad drove through once and liked what he saw. Guess what impressed him the most."

"What?"

"That not many kids had iPods or cell phones."

"Really?" I said. "That's weird."

Danh nodded.

"You know why?" I said. "It's because their parents don't have money for that stuff. It's not a choice. If they had money, they'd all have iPods and cell phones. Me too," I added.

"So you've lived in East Liberty your whole life?" Danh asked.

"Yeah," I said. "Dad went to East Liberty High, too. But I've traveled," I added, so I wouldn't seem like a hick. "I went to Paris once."

It turns out Danh had been to Paris too. And Barcelona. And Rome. And Istanbul. His dad liked to travel—I guess in between driving through dumpy towns like East Liberty.

"What happened to that 'No Bush, No War' sign in your front yard?" Danh asked. "That was cool."

"Someone stole it," I said. "If you thought it was cool, why didn't your family put out a sign too? We were the only ones."

Danh shook his head. "I don't know. Dad probably forgot."

After a few more hands of Pitch, we heard Mrs. Phan call out "dinner's ready" and we walked downstairs to a table crammed with food: a big fish on a platter, milky eyes in its head, a china bowl of steaming noodles, white rice, green beans, a huge bowl of salad. My first response was: ugh, fish. Stinky fish. And milky fish eyes are disgusting. But then I breathed in—and it smelled wonderful. I mean, really wonderful, fresh and sweet and sour at the same time. I hadn't seen or smelled a dinner I really wanted to eat since Mom left, and I suddenly felt starved, like I could eat that entire fish—eyes included—if they'd let me at it. Mr. Phan filled up my plate. It was amazing to see him cut the fish. Dad butchers everything, like the turkey he shreds every Thanksgiving, blaming the dull carving knife. After a couple of quick slices with a knife that definitely wasn't dull, Mr. Phan would lift up a perfect piece.

"Justin," Mr. Phan said, "Danh tells me you two have been biking to school together." He pronounced the name the Vietnamese way, "Yen."

I glanced at Danh.

"Yeah," I said. "It's been fun."

"I'm glad," Mr. Phan said.

I looked down to see Binh licking his chops, staring at me, head tilted mournfully to one side.

This time, Danh's father was the one with questions, about school, hobbies, what I liked to read. I could tell he was careful not to bring up my mother. Besides his difficulties with l's and r's, he was easy to understand. Mrs. Phan served cherry pie with ice cream for dessert. It was strange eating with them—formal and relaxed at the same time. I liked it. Danh and I were excused after I finished my second helping.

"We'll do the dishes tonight," Mr. Phan said to Danh. And to me: "We hope you come back soon."

"That fish," I said to Mrs. Phan as I got up from the table. "That was the best thing I've ever eaten. I didn't realize fish could taste . . . actually good."

She smiled. "We'll do this again," she said. "You can count on it."

———

"Before you go," Danh said, "I want to show you something."

"What?"

"Just follow me."

I followed him along a hall to a door that led to stairs going down. Danh switched on a light, and we trudged into a big, open basement smelling of fresh paint. A little exercise area with a Nordic Track was set up in one corner, a workbench with tools mounted on the wall in another corner. Danh walked to a section of wall that was bare except for a painting of a man in uniform, arms folded across his chest.

"Dad painted that," Danh said. "From a photograph."

It was a young soldier looking serious. Cocky and serious. Brown hair, dark eyes. Lifelike.

Danh took the painting down to reveal a little door behind it. "A fireproof cabinet," he said. "A lot of old houses have them." When Danh swung the door open, I expected to see something valuable, or at least interesting. What I saw was a folded gray cloth.

"What's that?" I asked.

"A blanket."

"Why do you keep a blanket here?"

"It's Dad's. The only thing he's got from Vietnam. It's what my grandmother wrapped him in when they escaped."

I felt I was supposed to say something, but didn't have any idea what. I wasn't sure why Danh wanted me to see this. I wasn't sure what it meant. I reached to touch the blanket, but Danh stopped me.

"Dad doesn't like anyone touching it."

"OK," I said. "OK." I bent low to examine the painting. "Who's the guy?"

"My grandfather."

"But he's white." I gulped. "I mean, not Vietnamese."

"Yeah, he was a soldier."

"An American soldier," I said. "Like my grandfather."

"My dad," Danh said, "I think he's a little ashamed. You know, of how he got born and all that."

"Is your grandfather alive?" I asked.

"We don't know."

Danh closed the door, rehung the painting, and we walked up the stairs without talking more. We said goodbye on the front porch.

And I thought as I walked to my house that Danh had just told me something important about himself and his family. That blanket. That painting. His grandfather. The fact that his father feels ashamed. And he trusted me to understand how important it was.

5

Monday

I FOUND OUT about Mom and Gerald because of a bird. A huge bird with a white head that flapped onto the branch of a dead tree across the road on a Sunday, late afternoon. It caught my eye as I passed the living room window. "A bald eagle!" I shouted, even though Mom and Dad were out shopping, and it was only me in the house. "Jesus Christ, a bald eagle! In East Liberty!"

I ran to the kitchen bookshelf for Mom's bird book, but it wasn't in its place next to *Wildflowers of the Eastern United States*. I raced around checking windowsills and countertops, then up to their bedroom. The bedroom window had a great view of the backyard bird feeder, which Mom filled every morning. I thought, OK, where would she toss the book? I couldn't see it anywhere. In a drawer? It must be, if it's out of sight. Mom's top drawer was halfway open, so I yanked it out, thinking she might have dropped the book there in a rush, but saw only a scattering of necklaces and earrings. I pulled out the second drawer: her underwear, so I slammed it shut. The third was stuffed with blouses. I jammed both hands in, out of desperation since there wasn't much chance she'd tossed it there, but that's where it was: *Birds of New York*. I raced downstairs, but too late: the bird had flown away. "White head, brown body," I said aloud. "Got to be a bald eagle!" When I opened Mom's book to the index, a folded sheet slipped out.

I scanned it. A joke? But this wasn't a joke Mom and Dad would ever play. It wasn't any kind of joke.

The writing was full of corny things a boyfriend would say, like "my sweetie" and "my soul mate." I tried to imagine everything the letter with its scribbled blue ink could be other than what it was. But it could only be one thing. I didn't know the guy who signed the letter "all my love, Gerald." I couldn't put a face to that name, which made me angry: how could there be this huge part of her life, this guy named Gerald that she fell in love with, who had nothing to do with me, a person I never could have imagined? It was a name connected to where she worked, along with a half dozen other names I'd half hear when she was talking about her job. I stuck the letter back in the book, ran upstairs, and tossed the book in the drawer.

In my room, I crawled under my bedcovers. I pressed a pillow over my face. Why would Mom save that letter, I wondered, then hide it in a drawer in the bedroom where she and Dad sleep? Did she write the same stupid things to Gerald? Did he hide her letter in some secret place in his own house? I wanted to wake up and discover that the whole sickening business was a dream, one of those crazy, impossible nightmares that I could laugh about when safely eating breakfast in our safe, normal, Gerald-free kitchen. A bald eagle started the whole thing. A stupid bald eagle.

I stayed in bed until I heard the front door open, and didn't move for the next hour. Then I heard my mother's voice calling me to dinner. I walked down the stairs like a sleepwalker. When she saw me, she knew immediately that something was wrong, asking a couple of times as we ate, "Do you feel OK, dear? Is anything the matter?" Dad, though, was oblivious. Somehow we got through dinner, and all I wanted was to be by myself in my room, but when Dad headed for the kitchen with a stack of dishes, I decided to say something. "Decided" isn't accurate. The words tumbled out.

"I saw a bald eagle today," I said.

"Really?" she said. "That's surprising. Maybe it was following the canal." She began stacking plates from the table.

"Yeah," I said. "But I wasn't sure. You know, if it was the real thing."

She turned to me, an anxious look on her face, and put down the plates she held.

"Did you find out?" she said.

That's when I said the real question on my mind.

"Why don't you love Dad any more?"

Her mouth opened a little, and she blinked a few times.

"What makes you say that?" she said quietly, gathering some dirty silverware. "Of course I love your father."

She glanced quickly at the kitchen, where I could hear water running.

"I found that letter," I said. "In the bird book in your drawer."

I thought she might ask the obvious question: why were you going through my drawer? But she didn't. She shifted her gaze to her plate.

"It's complicated," she said. "I do still love your father."

Then Dad walked in for a load of dishes.

"Justin," my mother said. "We can let you off dishwashing duty tonight. Why don't you start your homework?"

"My homework?"

I looked at Dad, who was surprised at my mother's announcement. He looked at her, then me, then her.

"Yes, your homework," she said quietly. "We'll give you a break tonight."

I stood up and left. But I wasn't in any mood for homework. I just lay on my messy bed staring at a crack that zigzagged across the ceiling. At one point I walked out to the landing, and heard their muffled voices in the living room. I half expected to hear shouting, Dad's anger rising to my room. Part of me wanted to hear angry voices. But they were quiet, eerily quiet—voices that might be having a normal conversation, though it couldn't be normal at all. I knew that she wanted me to go to my room so she could tell him. I'd given her no choice but to tell him. I thought about sneaking to the stairwell to listen, but didn't. I didn't want to know how she said it, or the details, or what Dad said to her. They even slept in their bedroom that night.

We had a "family meeting" around the kitchen table the next day, as soon as I was home from school. Mom did most of the talking, about how she and Dad still loved each other and loved me, how important our family was, how we would always be a "family" no matter what—but now she and Dad needed time apart to think things through, and so on. And it would all be for the best, and so on. Dad sat there catatonic, staring at his coffee cup while she talked.

I didn't say a word. I didn't look at Mom. I couldn't look at Dad, except for a glance now and again. I couldn't wait to get away.

A week later she moved out of our house and in with Gerald.

———

Except for the Sundays that I spent with Dad, for most of that first year after the separation I lived with Mom and Gerald in a big house on North Maple Street, with his sons Eddie and Phillip, seven and nine years old. I wasn't given a choice.

Gerald was Mom's age, early forties, and had gotten divorced two years earlier. His kids spent half the year with him, half in Tampa with their mother. Eddie and Phillip didn't like me from day one. I don't blame them. I acted grumpy and spent hours in my room building card houses, watching them collapse into a stupid heap, and feeling sorry for myself. Gerald's big house wasn't my house, and I didn't want to be there, even if there was a dishwasher, an answering machine, and a huge TV in something they called "the play room." Gerald asked if I wanted a cell phone—he could get one cheap on his family plan. I said no, I'm fine. I'm OK as I am. These people weren't my family, except for Mom. They were intruders into my life.

On a Sunday night in April, while I was watching TV and Eddie and Phillip were in bed, Mom and Gerald walked in with serious faces. Without asking, Gerald turned off the TV. Mom sat next to me on the couch.

"We have news," she said.

"Good news," Gerald said. "I hope you'll be pleased."

Mom told me that the Marietta plant in East Liberty was shutting down, that people would lose jobs, and how hard it was for anyone, no matter how qualified, to find a good job in this town.

"Dad's got a good job," I said.

"There's nothing here any more. But I got lucky," Gerald put in. "I'm getting transferred. And promoted." He smiled. "VP for Marketing." He put a hand on Mom's shoulder. "And your mother can continue working for me when we move."

"If that plant shuts down, it won't be good news for Donny Schill's dad," I said. "Or lots of other people."

"Of course not," Mom said. "For us though . . . ," and she thought about how to phrase what she had to say without the words *us* or *good*. "For Gerald and me, it's *exciting* news."

"We're moving to San Diego," Gerald said. "California."

"I know where San Diego is," I said.

"We're all going," Mom said. "You too."

I couldn't stand Gerald's smiling face, his hand clamped on Mom's shoulder as if they were posing for a photograph. I suppose that hand was *demonstrating* something. Something he wanted me to see. Didn't she understand? I was brought up in East Liberty. I was a sophomore in high school. Didn't I have a say? That sounded important, so I said it.

"Don't I have a say?"

"No," Gerald said.

Mom shot him a look. The *be quiet and behave* look.

"Of course you do," she said. "That's why we're having this conversation."

"What I mean," Gerald said, "is that you don't have a say in *my* job decision. I don't either. That's how the corporate world operates. Especially in the current business climate. In fact, I'm lucky. I'm luckier than several people in my division I could tell you about, people who won't be having the kind of family talk that we're having."

"I want to stay," I said. "Here in East Liberty. With Dad. I don't want to move to San Diego."

The skin on Mom's forehead turned blotchy, her eyes watered up, her lips tightened. At that moment I wanted to reach out to her. I wanted Gerald to melt into the carpet like that witch from *The Wizard of Oz*. I wanted to look down at a Gerald stain on the carpet next to his shiny black shoes.

"I'd like it if you came with us," she said.

"Does Dad know?"

"Yes," she said. "But I asked him not to say anything until we had this talk."

"Does he want me to stay with him?"

Mom took a deep breath. "Yes, he does."

"So I can if I want?"

Another deep breath. "I'd rather you came with us."

"But I can stay if I want?"

"Yes."

I loved her for saying that, because I'd heard that in any separation involving kids the mother gets her way, unless she's a crackhead or suicidal. And I felt this surge of love for Dad—because he wanted me to stay.

"But I'd like you to think about coming," she continued. "To think seriously about coming with us. You could still visit your father of course. Every school holiday you could visit. You'll make new friends in California and keep the friends that you have here."

"I don't need to think about it. I want to stay."

That was it. Mom and Gerald and his kids packed up and were gone to San Diego in a month, though it took half a year to sell Gerald's big house. Mom started calling me every Monday and Thursday at seven o'clock. The first four or five times, she cried a lot—she tried to hide it by saying she had a cold or allergy, but I could tell. After a month or so she could ask questions about my week without crying. And I'd ask about her week, and she'd say a few things. Pretty soon those phone calls began to seem almost normal. Except, of course, they weren't normal. And though I used to spend time trying to figure out what would make Mom leave Dad for Gerald, I never got the answer: Gerald didn't seem all that *demonstrative* as far as I could tell. I still don't have the answer. I wonder if it was something to do with me. Or with little Mike dying the way he did, without warning or reason: that definitely changed Mom—it changed all of us.

Sometimes I wonder what would have happened if that bald eagle hadn't flown south from the Adirondacks, following the canal to rest in a dead tree on a Sunday afternoon when I was passing the window. Or what would have happened if Mom had a better hiding place for her letter. Or if some instinct hadn't made me open that drawer to look for the book. Maybe everything would be different. Maybe everything would be exactly the same.

———

The phone rang a little after seven.

"Justin?" Her voice sounded quiet.

"Hi Mom."

"How are you?"

"Good."

"How's your week going?"

"OK."

"Tell me about what you've been doing."

"Went to school. Did homework. Watched TV. Took a walk with Dad."

"How is your father?"

I hated how she'd started calling Dad "your father."

"He's good."

"What did he make for dinner this week?"

"Pork chops. Spaghetti." I left out that the spaghetti was still in its can. I thought about telling her I'd just eaten a fantastic fish dinner at Danh's house, but decided not to.

"Any vegetables? Any greens?"

"Sure," I said. "Every meal. All the time."

We were quiet.

"Mom?" I said.

"Yes?"

"On Thursday I'm giving a presentation on World War II."

"That sounds interesting."

"On the Medal of Honor. I want to bring Grandpa's medal."

"You'll have to ask your father."

"I know."

"I'm not sure he'll like the idea."

"Yeah, I know."

"It's strange being here without you," Mom said from out of the blue. "I mean, difficult."

Then come home, I wanted to say. Come home and Dad will be different. I'll make sure he is. Just come home.

I knew she wanted me to ask how she was, how Gerald and Eddie and Phillip were doing. She wanted me to ask about the "difficult" thing she'd mentioned. But I couldn't.

We were quiet again. Finally we said goodbye.

Sometimes in bed before falling asleep, or when I'm awake before it's time to go down for breakfast, or at school in a study hall when I can't focus on what I'm reading, I think of things to tell her. Like if I saw a goldfinch or black-capped chickadee on one of my walks with Dad, because she'd taught me their names. Or if I got a 95% on a math quiz. But then, when the phone call comes, the list evaporates. Or if it's still in my head, it suddenly becomes a list belonging to someone else.

———

Loud voices woke me. The loudest was Dad's but I couldn't make out the words. I got out of bed. Outside my bedroom I heard Dad telling someone in a low, intense voice, to "stand up slowly."

I crept down the stairs and peeked around the corner. The ceiling light was on. Dad stood by the couch in his flannel pajamas. Bernie Schill, Donny's older brother, was kneeling on the carpet in blue overalls and a gray T-shirt. Next to him was our crappy DVD player, Dad's camera, our phone, and a ten gallon garbage bag stuffed half full. Dad was holding a flashlight in one hand and a gun in the other.

Bernie started blubbering. "It's not my fault. You gotta believe me. I'm not like this. It's just . . . I gotta find some fucking cash." His eyes were zipping all over the place. He started picking at the bald spot at the crown of his head.

"How many houses?" Dad asked.

"Three."

"Where?"

"Here. I mean, this street."

"You need to return everything. Right now. Everything goes back where you got it."

"OK," Bernie said. "I will, I promise. You know me."

"I thought I did," Dad said.

Bernie's bald spot was bleeding—I saw red on his finger-tips—and Dad must have seen it too because he said, sternly, "Stop picking that." And more quietly, "Keep your hands at your sides. Try to concentrate."

"I'm going to jail, aren't I?" Bernie said. "I'm completely fucked. More fucked than I've ever been and I've been really fucked."

"Get control of yourself," Dad said. "Go and return what you stole, and come back here. I'll make some breakfast, and we'll talk, and then you can go home. When did you last eat?"

"Don't remember," Bernie said. "Who needs to eat?"

"Everyone," Dad said. "And that includes you."

"Crank is what I need. I'm dying for it." Bernie said this as if he was a starved man talking about a hamburger.

"Jesus Christ," Dad said. "You need real food. Go and give back what you've stolen. That's the only way out of this mess. Come here when you're done, and you'll get the best breakfast you've ever had, I promise."

I watched Bernie stand unsteadily, and Dad—still holding the gun—walked him to the front door.

"I'm sorry," Bernie said. "I'm not myself. I'm . . . I'm some other person."

"Just return what you took and come back. It'll be OK."

Dad let him out, watched him walk to his pickup, then turned and with shoulders hunched rubbed his face and forehead with his free hand. When he looked up, he saw me crouched at the base of the stairs.

"My God, Justin. How long have you been there?"

"Did we just get robbed?"

"It's OK. He left everything, and he's returning what he stole from other people."

"Other people?"

"That's what he said. Three houses."

"I can't believe Bernie Schill robbed us. If he'd tried something, would you have shot him?"

Dad looked at the gun as if he couldn't figure out where it came from, though his finger was on the trigger. "It's Grandpa's Luger. There's no bullets. Doesn't even work." He set it on a chair. "Well, it did work, well enough to make Bernie pay attention."

Dad's face was shining—sweat, I guess. And he suddenly looked real tired. For a moment, he looked like an old man— or the old man he'd be in twenty years. "Help me put this stuff away," he said.

"Sure Dad," I said. I wanted to help, because I felt proud of him right then and glad he wanted my company.

We got to work emptying out the garbage bag, returning our DVD player to the cabinet, the camera and boom box to the cupboard. Finally we sat at the kitchen table and waited. Dad put on coffee. I made and drank hot chocolate.

"What's wrong with Bernie?" I asked.

"He's a methamphetamine user," Dad said. "The stuff's all over East Liberty, according to Jack Boland."

"Will he go to jail?"

"I hope not. He doesn't need jail. He needs help."

———

We waited for over an hour. Dad checked the kitchen clock, turned, and slammed his hand on the table—something I'd never seen him do before. "Bernie's made a mistake," Dad said. "A huge mistake. He should have come back. Now I've got no choice. I have to call Jack."

Dad made me go to my room. "Get some sleep," he said. "Excitement's over, and you've got school tomorrow. We still need to get up in the morning."

———

Twenty minutes later Jack Boland was in our living room. I was awake and heard the door open, then crept to the top of the stairs to listen.

"He's committed four felonies we know of," Boland said. "Probably more. And he's a meth addict. That's why he needs money. And he knows something about who's making and selling the stuff. Why did you let him go? What's the matter with you?"

"I thought he'd learned his lesson. I didn't just let him go. I talked to him."

"Because of you he's got an hour's head start and a pickup full of stolen property."

Boland got on the phone, barking out instructions to someone, and a minute later told Dad, "By now he's half way to Pennsylvania, or Massachusetts, or Canada." He shook his head. "And he'll drive through the night and the next day because he'll be stoked on meth. What the hell were you thinking?"

"I was thinking about his parents' dairy farm going bust and him getting laid off from the processing plant. And I gave him an F at the college. Then he dropped out. He was a different kid before things went sour. He kept saying he wasn't himself."

"So you felt sorry for him. Why does he steal from neighbors, people he's known all his life? He's a bad kid. Just like that Conklin kid, Wacko Conklin. You were that kid's champion too—even after he almost burned down the school. There isn't a mother who doesn't think her idiot son is an angel in disguise. But listen to me: if Bernie Schill shows up again in this town, I won't play nice. He's a lowlife drug addict who robbed my sister. He damn well knew that was Emily's house. The boy made a fool of me, and I swear to God he'll pay for it."

With that, Jack Boland stomped out. I'd never seen him so angry. He actually slammed the door. He and my dad have a history in this town—they were best friends in high school—which is maybe why they can get angry at each other.

It turns out that Bernie not only didn't return the stuff he'd stolen from other houses, but he'd also kept fifty dollars we didn't know he'd taken out of Dad's money jar in the kitchen. He just got in his pickup and drove out of town.

6

Tuesday

WHEN DAD KNOCKED ON MY DOOR to wake me for school, I was at the end of a dream that spun off of something that really happened one Saturday in August while I was staying with Mom and Gerald in San Diego. The real part started with a day trip to Tijuana. None of us had been there, which explains why Mom and Gerald didn't know Tijuana is one of the most revolting places on earth. Their idea was to go shopping for cheap Mexican stuff. But the streets were full of Mexicans missing hands or legs, with terrible scars and skin diseases, yelling at you to buy something, or just begging. It started as soon as you crossed the border. Which meant that to make it through the day, you had to stop being a decent person as soon as you entered Tijuana. We walked up and down a wide avenue, peeking into shop windows, getting accosted at every step by people whose lives were too sad to even think about. It was incredibly hot. Besides all the general bad smells in Tijuana, the air actually *smelled* hot. To escape, we ducked into a café, taking a table as far from the sidewalk as we could. But even the waiters tried to sell us stuff: scribbled drawings of our "happy" family, or Polaroid photographs they'd snap while we weren't looking. Gerald bought a snapshot of us sitting around the table—that set him back ten bucks. On my way to the disgusting men's room, a busboy tried to sell me a joint.

Mom and Gerald had been bickering ever since we walked by the first gauntlet of beggars. She'd given them coins and dollars until she ran out, because she has a hard time not being human. Then she asked Gerald for money.

"Stop," he said. "Just stop. I'm not giving money to Mexican beggars. You might as well flush it down the toilet. What difference will a dollar make in their lives?"

"I'm not saying it'll make a difference," Mom said. "But I can't just walk by these people."

"Yes you can. Look straight ahead and keep moving. One foot in front of the other. That's how you walk by. It's easy."

Gerald had that non-human thing down pretty good.

Then Mom started picking on the fact that Gerald hadn't packed sunscreen, his only assignment. They could have bought sunscreen at one of the thousand sunscreen shops in Tijuana, but it bugged Mom that they had a tube already open at the house. Gerald was complaining about the heat, and wanted a beer. Mom told him there'd be no beer drinking this early. They continued on like that. I finally couldn't take any more. I told Mom I wouldn't sit in that tourist trap café with them bickering. I was going for a walk. They argued with me, but I countered that "I can take care of myself. I'm not stupid. I'm not a child." Mom finally said OK, as long as I kept to the main avenue and didn't go more than three blocks in any direction. She made Gerald give me four dollars for water. "Keep hydrated!" she shouted as I walked away.

Ragged Tijuana kids ran to me and begged, holding out their battered Styrofoam cups. Adult hawkers called out *hey Amigo!*, reaching to shake my hand like we were long-lost friends. But mostly they left me alone, figuring I was too young to have much to spend or give. At the first intersection I turned left off the main avenue. Three or four doors down, I saw a bookstore that sold comic books. Half the titles in the window were in Spanish, half in English. I figured I'd use my dollars to buy a couple in Spanish because Rusty might think they were cool. They were yellow with age. Nothing held my interest until I shifted to the right side of the window. Here the covers showed women with bare breasts, little nipples in the middle of each large circle. Then a door to the left of the bookstore opened and a girl my age walked out. She stood there, blinking as if surprised by the sunlight. She turned a little, smiled, tilted her head towards the dark doorway. I froze. She wore a white blouse and short green skirt. She was pretty. She could have been a girl in East Liberty High, except for the darker skin and too short skirt. A red, half-inch scar stood out on her cheek.

"You come in?" she said. "You want date?"

It took a minute to figure out what she meant. "No," I said. "I'm OK."

A man walking down the street—fat and short, in his forties, wearing checkered shorts and a polo shirt—stopped when he reached us.

"How much?" he asked in a southern American drawl.

"Twenty-five," the girl said.

"How much for both?" With fingers and thumbs he made little circles, which he set over his eyes. "Watch," he said. "Me watch both."

She frowned and cocked her head, letting him know she didn't understand.

"Both. Watch both." He pointed to her, then me.

She laughed. She opened her mouth and laughed loudly, and I saw she was missing a front tooth.

"No," she said. "For you, just me."

"OK," he said. "Ten dollars for you."

"OK."

They went inside and shut the door. I examined the closed door, which had a long brownish smear running down the middle. I was alone on the street now, and moved to the left end of the display window to look over familiar heroes: Spider-Man, the

Green Lantern, Superman, Wonder Woman, Batman, Captain Marvel. There were even World War II comics, with Nazis pointing machine guns at women wearing almost no clothes. At that moment everything around me, and everything in my life, seemed wrong. My legs felt wobbly, and I wished I could drop down in a heap on the filthy street and not go anywhere or do anything, not have to stand, not have to walk, not even breathe. But instead I started trudging slowly up to the main avenue. A block to the right I saw my mother, her head jerking this way and that. Gerald, I supposed, was scouting for me too.

That's what really happened, but in my dream I didn't walk up the street to see my mother. I didn't catch hell about being irresponsible and not following instructions. In the dream it was me, not the guy in the checkered shorts, who followed the girl through the doorway. We walked up a staircase, first her, then me, and continued through another door. But that door opened into my own messy bedroom in East Liberty. Instead of the Mexican girl, it was Jamie Peterson who flopped down on my bed, wearing a white blouse and short green skirt. The scar above Jamie's eyebrow was the same as the one on the Mexican girl's cheek. It wasn't strange that she was in my bedroom. Jamie was serious and matter-of-fact, the same as when she'd told me to bring Grandpa's medal and my notes to school. But then she turned to face me and started laughing, just as the Mexican girl had laughed—an open-mouth, loud laugh from where she was lying on the bed. And I saw then that she, like the Mexican girl, was missing a front tooth.

———

Dad was in a grumpy mood as he pushed scrambled eggs around in the frying pan with a spatula. He was humming but the humming was deep and tight, like he'd strained his vocal chords.

"I can't believe we got robbed last night," I said.

"We didn't," Dad replied. "Remember? He left everything and we put it all away."

"Yeah, but he kept everyone else's stuff, right?"

"I know," Dad said as he set eggs and toast in front of me.

I guessed the robbery wasn't something he wanted to talk about.

"Did you clean your room and make your bed?"

"No time."

"Get to it this morning. Make time. We're not going to live like slobs who can't take care of themselves."

"OK," I said, irritated at his irritated tone. Was it his business if I liked a messy room? Wasn't it my room? Wasn't I a person like him? Did I bug him about his bedroom? I hadn't done anything to deserve his irritation.

After breakfast, I dressed, got my backpack organized, and decided to see if Danh had left for school. When I knocked, his dad opened the door in a suit and tie, like he'd just come home from church.

"Danh!" he shouted into the stairwell. "Justin's here!" and in a second Danh was bounding down the stairs.

On the way to school, we biked side by side, and I told Danh about Bernie Schill, and Dad pointing Grandpa's Luger at him. Danh was wide-eyed trying to imagine my dad with a gun. It felt good telling him about it.

"Your dad's amazing," Danh said. "I mean, trying to help a guy high on drugs who stole from you is amazing. And he had a gun. He actually pointed a real, live gun that could kill a person."

"Yeah," I said. "Sometimes I think he tries too hard, always thinking he can help."

"What's wrong with that?" Danh asked.

Danh had a point, but I wasn't yet ready to give my dad a pass. Trying to get Bernie to return the stuff he'd stolen reminded me of the time Richie Ryan and I got caught smashing pumpkins on

Halloween. We weren't trying to be bad, we just liked the way the pumpkins sounded, thumping and splattering on sidewalks. What did we know? Dad made me go back to each house and apologize. Six houses, and of course everyone was home. "You'll learn a lesson apologizing for what you did," Dad told me. "And you'll get to spend time with neighbors." Spend time with neighbors? He made it sound like a block party.

"I bet your dad must have some interesting stories," I said to Danh, to get off the subject of my own dad. "About leaving Vietnam as a kid."

"He won't talk about that," Danh said, "no matter how much I ask. All he'll say is, 'It's complicated.' So I guess some bad things happened."

We stopped by the old Jordan house to check on the cat family. The first thing I noticed was that the purple martin mansion had fallen off its pole. One side was caved in, and where it had been attached, the pole was splintered.

"How'd that happen?" Danh asked. "The wind?"

"A baseball bat is my guess," I said. "One big swing."

"Why would someone do that?" Danh looked worried. "And where are the kittens?"

We found them under the porch, a kitten-heap, sleeping.

"Do you think something happened to the mom?" Danh asked.

"Must be out hunting," I said. I had to just about yank Danh away. "Come on," I told him. "They won't look any different tomorrow. We'll be late if we don't get going."

"I'd like to be inside that pile of kittens," Danh said as we got on our bikes. "I'd like to be right in the middle."

———

All through my morning classes and in gym, my lunch with Jamie was constantly on my mind. Finally it was near twelve, and

I was heading to the cafeteria. This time I didn't dump my lunch in the garbage. I saw Del at the furthest back table. If he saw me, or cared about me in any way, he didn't show it. He didn't glance in my direction. I don't matter, I thought. I'm invisible again. I don't exist again. So the cops didn't figure out it was Del driving. It'll all go away. None of it matters. Everyone will just forget.

Jamie and Danh were at the table, already eating.

"Let's see it," Jamie said when I sat down.

"See what?"

"The medal."

"Oh God," I said. "I was so rushed this morning I forgot. I'm really sorry."

"I should have reminded you," Danh blurted out. "I was going to, but I forgot." He looked like he was about to punch himself in the head.

"You'll remember to bring it to class tomorrow," Jamie said. "Right, Justin?"

"I guess so."

"You won't forget?"

"I won't."

"Tell your dad to remind you," Danh said. "My dad writes everything on a list that he posts on the refrigerator."

"I'll remember. Don't worry." And I thought, how the hell do I convince Dad? He won't even show it to friends who visit the house.

We spent the rest of lunch organizing the presentation, with Danh listening in. When the bell rang, we hadn't finished.

"I've got an idea," Jamie said. "Come to my house after school. We'll finish then."

"OK." In case she didn't hear or might misinterpret me, I said it again, more loudly. "OK."

"We're on Slate Road, number 301, a white colonial. Can you stay for dinner? I'm sure Mom won't mind."

"OK," I said, swallowing hard. I felt as if my vocabulary had boiled down to that one word.

"I'll tell Dad," I said, to prove I had more words at my command. "Then I'll bike over."

"Got to run," Jamie said. "Marty and I are prepping a biology presentation in study hall." She picked up her tray and rushed to the conveyor belt and the door.

Danh immediately started up about Jamie in a whisper, then as he got excited, pretty loudly. "She just asked you over to her house! Is that a date? I can't believe that happened. You've got a date with Jamie Peterson. Did that really happen, or am I dreaming?"

"It's not a date. And can you lower your voice?"

"It *is* a date. It's a 'study-date.' That counts."

"It won't be a date."

Danh frowned for a moment, then quietly said, "I wish I could be you."

"You wouldn't want that," I said. "Believe me."

Danh shut up then, but he had planted the date idea in my head, and I couldn't shake it. Was this a date? Did Jamie think it was a date? Could it turn into a date?

———

After school let out, Danh said he needed to stay for chess club, so I walked by myself to the bike rack. At the school's front door I ran into Rusty and Fred, heading toward their buses.

"Hey," Rusty said. "Haven't seen you around."

Fred, as usual, was more direct. "How come you're eating lunch with Jamie Peterson and that Vietnamese kid?"

"You mean Danh."

"Who?"

"Danh Phan. I've been eating lunch with Danh."

"Yeah, him."

"We're working on a history presentation."

"Two days in a row?" Rusty said.

"Jamie wants to be sure it's good."

"She does?" Rusty said this as if he couldn't imagine someone wanting to do well on a presentation.

"Yeah, she's really smart."

"Are you . . . are you like, seeing her?"

"No."

"Too bad," Rusty said. "I mean, that's definitely too bad."

"She's not seeing anyone, at least not that I know of."

"Really?" Rusty said. "I thought girls who look like her are always seeing someone."

"Apparently not."

"Hey," he said next, "the Yanks are playing the Orioles Saturday. Want to watch? Fred's coming over. Game starts at noon."

"Yeah," I said. "Sure." Then I thought for a second. "OK if Danh comes too?"

Fred and Rusty looked at each other. Fred shrugged.

"Fine by me," Rusty said.

"Sure," Fred added. "Why not?"

———

I felt great biking home, with dinner at Jamie's coming up and Del not noticing me at all in the cafeteria. And though I didn't much like watching baseball on TV, I was happy that Danh could come along for the Saturday game. I took my time biking, since it was a sunny afternoon, and detoured through Watson Park to cruise by the big old maples in full color. A few people were walking dogs and some mothers pushed baby strollers, but mostly I had the park to myself. As I veered left towards home I was surprised to see a big concrete arch—the entrance to Oak View cemetery. I shouldn't have been surprised, since I'd known that cemetery all my life, but it's where little Mike is buried, and I'd blocked it from my mind. I'd never visited Mike's grave by myself—it was always with Mom and Dad on the anniversaries of his birth and the day he died. I biked through the arch onto the main road—Serenity Way—and continued up the hill.

I knew the grave was somewhere up ahead, but every time we visited I couldn't see his among all the other gray gravestones until Dad or Mom announced, "here it is." All those dead people in rows and rows was too much to take in. I was breathing hard from pumping up that hill and thought I'd missed it. Then my eyes locked onto his name so suddenly I almost fell off my bike. I set the bike down and walked over. Under "Michael James Lyle" were the words "son and brother." I was glad my parents didn't put anything sappy on—like those angels or teddy bears you sometimes see. The grass on his grave had just been mowed—probably for the last time this season. A vase of fresh flowers sat in front of the gravestone—daisies—which meant that Dad had visited.

I stood in front of Mike's grave, not knowing what to do.

"I'm sorry," I said, finally. "I'm just really sorry."

———

At home when I opened the front door I could hear Dad humming while cooking in the kitchen. It was the bouncy humming Dad does when he's feeling good.

"Hey, Just," he said as I walked in. He was wearing that stupid cardigan.

"Dad," I said, "Jamie wants me to go to her house to work on our presentation. I can bike over. She asked me to stay for dinner."

"Sure, that's fine. That's great news. Stay as late as you want." He was smiling ear to ear. "I've got news too."

"Things better at the college?"

"No, bad as ever, maybe worse. But Jack Boland ID'd the plate for that car."

"That car?"

"The one those juvenile delinquents were driving. Turns out it's Fulton Blake's car, and Jack says the driver has to be his son, Delroy. Anyway, Jack had a talk with Fulton, who told Jack that he'd take care of it—he'd teach his kid how to behave."

"Really?" I felt like throwing up.

"Jack asked if I wanted to file charges. But I said that if the boy gets disciplined by his dad, that's good enough."

"That's good enough?" I said. "That's good enough?"

"What's wrong? You're not a friend of this Delroy kid are you?"

"No."

"Like I said, I'm not filing charges, so it's no big deal. But maybe now the boy will change his ways and straighten out. He might get some parental supervision."

Dad turned down the heat on the burner, and stirred something thick and brownish.

Change his ways! I thought. Parental supervision! No big deal! I screamed the last three words in my head again: *no big deal!* I went to my room. I flopped on the bed. "Thanks to you, Dad," I said aloud, "the big deal is just beginning." Why couldn't he know that piss on an ugly sweater is nothing compared to what happens when someone like Del Blake gets involved in your life? Was Dad living on some other planet? And all this is starting when I'm getting to know Jamie, when we're maybe having a date, or at least a study-date.

The presentation! The Medal of Honor! I ran into Dad's bedroom, pulled open the top drawer of his chest of drawers. I expected to see the medal all by itself in the empty drawer. Didn't he say top drawer? Instead, I saw letters, a couple hundred spread out, all the same size. All with Dad's name on them, all the same handwriting. The return address was Helen DeReuter, 116 State Street, Binghamton.

I took out a page and read "Dearest Matt." I thought: Dad isn't *Dearest* any more, is he, Mom? Now, he's *Dear*, as in "Dear John." Gerald had become her *Dearest*. I tossed the letter back in the drawer. Dad and Mom had been in love. She'd written him these letters. She must have written every day for a while, maybe twice a day. She called him "Dearest Matt." And Dad kept them all. Even after Mom moved to San Diego, he kept them all—in a drawer, just like Mom kept her special letter in a drawer. I started to laugh, the sort of laugh that doesn't make any noise because you keep your lips tight, laugh through your nose, and shake your head as you do it.

Until that moment I had no idea that these letters existed. I plunged my hands into that lake of letters. I pulled out what I thought was a toy, but it was too heavy for a toy. It was Grandpa's Luger, the one Dad had pointed at Bernie Schill. That's where he kept it—under Mom's letters. Odd place to hide a gun, I thought. It was old and worn, especially the wooden handle. Even close up, it didn't look real, with that super thin black barrel. But the more I stared at it, the more I liked it, especially the crescent moon silver trigger. I thought about how the Germans had the coolest weapons in the old war movies my friend Richie and I used to watch. I set it back in the drawer and felt around underneath the letters some more. My hands closed on a hard box and then a small book. I took both out, closed the drawer, and ran to my room.

At my desk I opened the box. The medal, attached to a blue silk ribbon, was exactly as I remembered from when Dad last let me see it. An eagle perched over the word "Valor." A green wreath wrapped around a five-pronged star. In the middle, the goddess of war. As soon as I saw that eagle I thought about the eagle in the tree the day I found Gerald's letter. I stuffed the box under my pillow.

Then I opened the little book to the first sentence on the first page, dated March 6, 1942, and read, "Downtown Buffalo. Army physical. Classified 1-A." The next entry, May 31, 1942, had just one word: "Enlisted." It was my grandfather's diary about his years in the war—a diary I didn't know existed just as I didn't know Mom's letters to Dad existed.

I checked my watch. I had to get going to Jamie's house. I slipped the diary next to the Medal of Honor under my pillow and sprinted down the stairs.

7

Tuesday

THE WHITE COLONIAL that Jamie said I'd find halfway down Slate Road had a wide front porch with a swinging love seat at one end. It was more like a small mansion than a house, and reminded me of the parachute palace on Route 8 that Dad complained about on our walk, though Jamie's house looked a lot older. On the front lawn was a maple with the reddest leaves I'd ever seen—as if someone had injected dye into the tree. "Red" didn't do those leaves justice. They needed a special name, like "scarlet" or "vermillion." An *ornamental* tree is what Dad would have called it, saying the word with disdain. I stood in front of the brass doorknob and took a deep breath before ringing the bell. After the second ring, Jamie opened up. "Hi," she said matter-of-factly. "Come in." I followed her down a hall to a room where her father sat in an easy chair, reading a newspaper and holding a squat glass with a yellowish drink. Against the far wall, a huge TV showed the local news with the sound off. "This is Justin," she said. Her father looked up, checked me out, nodded, and went back to reading. "This way," Jamie said, and led me to the kitchen to meet her mother, wearing tight black pants and a fuzzy sweater and diamond earrings. Her blonde hair, parted in the middle, curved perfectly around her face to her shoulders.

"You've got an hour, dear," she said to Jamie. "I'll call you."

I followed Jamie down another hall into a large, open room she called the study, with a thick rug, a couch, a mahogany desk with a computer and printer, and bookshelves built into the wall and packed full of what looked like encyclopedias. Jamie spread her papers and our World War II books on the floor, and we got to work. In a way it reminded me of being on the floor with Richie all those years ago, except this time surrounded by papers and books instead of toy soldiers. And my friend was a girl I hardly knew, not a boy I'd known my whole life. What we were doing wasn't at all a game for Jamie—it was serious work: researching in our books and on the web, organizing notes, making an outline, rehearsing. For a study-date, it was all study and no date.

"So can we meet tomorrow at lunch?" Jamie said at the end of our second run-through. "For some tweaking."

"OK," I said. "OK." And then, for emphasis, "OK."

Dinner at the Petersons' was an opposite experience from the one at the Phan house. There was a white tablecloth, linen napkins, matching cutlery, with a steak placed in the middle of each white plate, the biggest on Mr. Peterson's plate, the next biggest on Mrs. Peterson's, down to the smallest, on my plate. And we all had steak knives—really big steak knives. Red wine had been poured in three glasses, soda in two. Mr. Peterson sat at one end of the table, Mrs. Peterson at the other. Jamie and I were next to each other in front of the sodas. Then a guy walked in and sat across from me. He looked like Del, if Del cleaned himself up and wore a polo shirt and khaki pants. He took ear buds out and stuffed them in a pocket.

"This is Jamie's brother Tony," Mrs. Peterson said.

"Hi," I said.

Tony nodded at me, and gulped down half his wine.

Bowls of mashed potatoes and green beans were passed around, and we started eating.

"So," Mrs. Peterson said, "are you two finished studying for that exam?"

"It's a presentation," Jamie said, "not an exam."

"We're finished," I put in. "We'll look at it once more tomorrow during lunch."

"Could you pass the wine?" Tony said to his dad.

Mr. Peterson continued eating as if Tony hadn't spoken. When he wiped his lips with his napkin, I saw a flash of red against the cream of the linen. He cut a portion of meat, put it in his mouth, chewed. I could see a red crease on his lower lip, which he licked every now and again. After every lick, the crease would clear, then turn bright red again.

"You're Matthew Lyle's son," Mr. Peterson said suddenly. It was the first time, after that nod in the TV room, that he acknowledged my existence.

"Yes."

"I knew your father when I was in school here."

"Dad," Jamie said. "Your lip is bleeding."

"Dry skin," he said, and wiped the blood off with his napkin.

"May I be excused?" Tony said to his mother. He'd eaten half the steak but left everything else. His wine glass was empty.

"Where are you going?"

"Where I always go," Tony said. "Nowhere." The smirk on his face was exactly like one you'd see on Del's face. "This town's so beat there's nowhere to go. How about I go back to Brooklyn Heights?"

"Tony is taking time off from college," Mrs. Peterson said. "He's at home this year."

"I'm forced to live in the land that time forgot," Tony said, "because I got kicked out of Hofstra."

Mr. Peterson pointed his steak knife at Tony. "That's enough. We have a guest. We keep our dirty laundry private." He picked up his wine glass, sipped, licked blood off his lip, and refilled.

Jamie's mother sighed. "Yes, Tony, you may leave."

When he'd gone, she turned to me. "Tony was at Hofstra for six months, then joined us in East Liberty, but he misses our neighborhood in Brooklyn Heights."

"He got what he deserved," Mr. Peterson said.

Nobody said anything to that, so I filled the silence.

"Do you ever . . ." I said. Everyone looked at me, but I'd lost the end of my sentence.

"Do you ever . . . go back to visit?"

"We live here now," Mr. Peterson said. "There's no going back. There's no point." He patted his lip again with his napkin.

"Tell us about yourself," Mrs. Peterson said. "What do you like to do outside of school?"

I froze up. Me? What was there to tell? Nothing, I thought to myself. Nothing to tell. I'm nothing, with nothing to tell.

"What I like," I said, "is."

Mrs. Peterson frowned.

I took a deep breath and started again.

"What I like is . . . playing chess." As soon as I'd said the words, I wanted to take them back. Chess was Danh's game, not mine.

"Really?" Mr. Peterson said. "How'd you learn the game?"

"From my dad."

"Has he been playing a while?"

Now that the lying started, I didn't know how to stop. "I think he played in high school."

Mr. Peterson cleared his throat. "In high school? Really?"

"I think so."

"I knew your father in high school."

I nodded.

"Are you a fan of Vladimir Kramnik?"

"I'm not sure. Who's he?"

"The world chess champion."

I saw the smirk on his face, a cousin of the one on Tony's face and Del's face, and hurriedly answered, "Yeah, he's great."

"What did you think about the match in Switzerland?"

"I missed that one."

Now the blood was pooling on Mr. Peterson's lip because he hadn't licked it while he talked.

"You're a chess fan and you missed the world championship?"

"Dad," Jamie said. "You can't expect Justin to know everything about chess. He only said he likes the game."

"Not everything," Mr. Peterson said. "But the world championship. . . ."

"We don't get cable," I said. "My dad. . . ." I didn't know where I was going but forged ahead. "Dad thinks there's too much junk on TV."

"I followed every move. Thought it was an amazing match. Not junk at all. And you're telling me you don't have cable television?"

"Dad," Jamie said. "Your lip. It's gross."

He licked it clean with three swipes.

I was desperate to get off the subject. "I like to read."

"Read?" Mrs. Peterson said. She was surprised. "What sort of reading?"

"About World War II."

"They got that history wrong," Mr. Peterson said. "At least in the standard books."

"Dear," said Mrs. Peterson, "can we not talk about politics at the dinner table?"

His eyes glazed over, and he went about cutting up the rest of his steak.

"What does your father do?" Mrs. Peterson asked. "For work?"

"He teaches," I said. "At the community college."

"And what does he teach?"

"English."

"I always thought Matt would go places," Mr. Peterson said. "Nothing wrong with teaching, but I thought he'd be a lawyer, maybe get into business."

We're not hicks, I wanted to say. We go places, we do things. But of course I kept quiet.

We ate for a while, with no one talking. Then Jamie and her mom cleared off the dishes, and her mom brought a lemon meringue pie from the kitchen. Jamie's dad returned to the subject of chess, talking about how in college he'd considered playing professionally. At any moment I expected him to quiz me on strategy.

"Another slice?" Mrs. Peterson asked.

"No thanks. I should be heading back." I forced down a last bite of that too-sweet pie. "I have homework."

My stomach was in knots. I thought that if Mr. Peterson licked his lip one more time I'd puke all over that perfect white tablecloth.

"Can I use your bathroom?" I asked.

"Of course," Mrs. Peterson said. "Down the hall on your left."

The bathroom was spotless, all gleaming porcelain and pale blue tiles. It wasn't just a toilet and sink but a big room, with bath and shower and a white wicker chair, matching wicker table with a spread of magazines about wines, recipes, modern houses. Who takes a shower in a hall bathroom? I wondered. I splashed water over my face and stared into the mirror. I didn't like what I saw: a pimple at my left temple, short brown hair, brown eyes. I smiled. I examined my lips: no cracks, no blood. I wrinkled my nose. I stretched the skin above and below my eyes, then pulled my lips to make different faces. Now my stomach felt better.

In the dining room, the dessert dishes had been cleared. Mr. Peterson was gone. Jamie didn't look happy.

"Goodbye, Justin," Mrs. Peterson.

"You have a great family," I said to Jamie on the front porch. "That was a great dinner." I was about to say "I had a great time," but caught myself. Great, great, great, great, great I chanted inside my head, to flush the word from my system.

Now that I was alone with Jamie without a presentation to rehearse, I didn't have an excuse to stay, but didn't want to leave. I had to fight back the urge to blurt out everything, tell Jamie I'd stolen the medal and Grandpa's diary from Dad's bedroom, that I was scared that Tommy DeSantis and Del would beat me up at school the next day for getting them in trouble, that I didn't play chess and had never heard of Vladimir Kramlick. It was all bubbling up. The sun had set, leaving red streaks spread along the horizon, and storm clouds were starting to gather. In the yard, I could make out those creepy scarlet maple leaves, now darker.

"Do you go to church?" Jamie asked. "I mean, regularly?"—a question came from nowhere.

"Yes," I said. "Because Dad likes to."

"Why?"

"I don't know—I never asked. It's not like he talks about God or goes to any church events except services. But he never misses a Sunday and always puts an envelope on the collection plate. Maybe it's habit—you know, doing it because it feels strange to stop. Not that there's many people who go anymore—it's usually three quarters empty."

"I wish we'd go," Jamie said.

This surprised me. "Really?"

"We're supposed to be Episcopalians, but my parents won't take me. They've always got some excuse. And of course Tony would never go. I admire people who are looking for something more than . . . than what we do every day."

She walked across the porch to the love seat, and motioned me to sit next to her.

"I've been wondering how Del got to be so mean," I said, since his meanness was something we'd experienced together—unlike church.

"He was born that way," Jamie said with conviction. "Before we moved here I'd see Del once a year at a family reunion. And every year he got stranger and stranger—quieter, but not in a good way. We stopped going to those after Aunt Sally died—she was Dad's sister, and Del's mom. So even though we're living in East Liberty now, we don't see Del's family at all, which is fine with me. He's not stupid, but he uses his intelligence to hurt people. I hate him. I hate the way he treats everyone as if they owe him money, or as if they're something to scrape off the bottom of his shoe. I hate being related to him. His father keeps calling here. I think he's asking Dad for money. Mom says all the Blakes are lowlife."

I heard Jamie's dad's voice in the house, yelling. The front door opened, Tony rushed out and slammed it shut. "Oh," he said, seeing us. "Sorry."

"It's OK," Jamie said.

He looked around the porch.

"Stay if you want," Jamie told him. "Join us."

"No thanks." He hesitated, then walked back in the house.

"Does your family have secrets?" Jamie asked me.

"We used to," I said. "And probably still have some."

"My family's completely screwed up," Jamie said, whispering intensely. "Worse than anyone knows." She turned away as she said the next words. "I think my dad's having an affair."

"Why do you say that?"

She shook her head. "Don't you see how my mom's acting? It's all fake. All surface and show. I have no idea what's really going on in her head. And Dad's mind is somewhere else. He's out late most nights. Something's going on that no one talks about. Of course, most things that go on in my family we don't talk about."

"My mom had an affair," I said. I don't think I'd ever before used the word "affair." It belonged to another language, to people who lived in big cities, or in parachute palaces.

"Is that why your parents split up?"

I nodded. "She and the guy moved away together."

"Where?"

"San Diego."

"Did you want to go with them? At least there's movie theaters in San Diego. And bookstores."

"I didn't want to leave Dad. And I like it here. My friends are here."

"Yeah," she said. "Danh is great. He doesn't try to be anyone except himself. I respect that."

We were quiet again.

"Why can't they just be honest?" Jamie said this so loudly I almost jumped off the seat. "Why can't they tell the truth?"

"I don't know," I said. "I'm really sorry. I mean, I hope it's not true that your dad's cheating on your mom."

She looked me straight in the eyes. "I hope it *is* true."

"Why?"

"Because I want him to leave."

"How come?"

"You wouldn't understand. You've got something like a normal family." She paused. "I mean, you had a normal family."

"I had a little brother," I said.

"You did? What happened?"

"He died at two months. One of those crib deaths."

"I'm so sorry." Jamie looked at me closely. "When was that?"

"Eight years ago. I was sleeping in the same room when it happened. I don't know if he cried out. If he did, I didn't hear. Mom boxed up and moved everything of little Mike's out of our bedroom the week after he died. Then, his crib disappeared—thrown away or given away I guess, though no one said anything to me. One morning it was there, and when I went to bed that night it was gone. Now it's like he never existed. But he did exist. I remember him. I remember his face."

"You can't blame yourself," Jamie said. "You didn't do anything wrong."

"But if I'd heard something, maybe I could have yelled for my mom and dad."

"No," she said. "You've got to stop that kind of thinking. You can't blame yourself. That's what I tell myself every day about my own family."

Then Jamie started talking really fast. "Tony's angry most of the time. When he's not, he's depressed, drinking by himself in his room, smoking pot. I smell it on him in the morning. He's just out of it most of the time."

I guess things had been bubbling up in Jamie too.

"And with Mom and Dad everything's about money. There's never enough. Sometimes I feel like I can't take it, that I'll just completely lose it. That one morning I won't be able to get out of bed."

I was suddenly aware of Jamie's shoulder brushing mine as she talked. Every time one of us moved, the whole swinging seat moved, and our shoulders and arms rubbed back and forth.

"Do you know," Jamie said, "that you're the first boy who's ever been in my house? That's because of Dad. 'Control freak' doesn't begin to describe him. I can't believe how he treated you at dinner." She took a deep breath, and exhaled slowly.

"You're nice," she said next. "You listen, and you're honest. I'm glad you came over." Then she leaned back, and stopped talking.

Should I kiss her, I wondered. Is this the moment? Is this how a kiss happens? Is it what I'm supposed to do? I couldn't read her expression. She might be expecting it; she might be horrified if I tried.

"I should get back," I said. I checked my watch.

"Yeah, I need to do some math," Jamie said.

And that was it.

———

I was home by a little after eight, hung up my jacket, yelled a quick "hi" to Dad, ran up the stairs to my room, and flopped on the bed. I felt the world spinning, the world and me spinning together. My heart was pounding fast. I hated myself for not kissing Jamie. I was too cowardly. I hated my mom, but desperately needed her to come home. I hated Dad, and wished he'd stop telling me to clean my room. I wished I could talk to someone about what was swirling in my head. I thought about phoning Danh, but it was too late.

I heard Dad's knock on my door.

"I'm doing homework," I shouted.

"Can I come in for a minute?"

I went to my desk chair and opened my math book.

"OK."

Dad came in and sat on my bed. As I swiveled to face him, I thought, would he somehow move the pillow and see the medal and diary underneath?

"Did Mom phone last night?" he asked.

"Isn't that when she always phones?"

I could see Dad thinking, should I call him on that, or let it go? He let it go.

"How is she?"

"Fine."

"Was it a good talk?"

"It was great."

"I'm glad," he said.

He glanced around, about to comment on my messy desk, the unmade bed, the clothes piled on the floor, when we heard a loud thump on the front door. Then the doorbell rang, not once but six or seven times fast, like a hammer. Then more thumping.

"Who the heck is that?" Dad said. "Pounding the door this time of night?"

"Don't answer," I said. "You don't have to answer."

"Of course I'll answer," Dad said, which is what I knew he'd say, and he stood up from the bed.

"Tell them I'm not home!" I yelled after him from the top of the stairs, because I was sure that pounding fist belonged to Del. "Don't open the door!"

But it was too late. I heard a loud, gruff voice. "You're the one," the voice boomed. "You told that cop Boland to bother me."

"That's right," Dad said. "I spoke with Officer Boland. Your son got himself in trouble."

"Next time, call me direct. I'll take care of Del myself, my own way. I don't need a cop getting in my business."

"There shouldn't be a next time," Dad said.

"I'm saying that if Boland ever comes to my house again, I'll know who sent him. And I'll take care of you real good. You gotta learn to keep things to yourself. You understand?"

"You should leave," Dad said. "You're about to get yourself into serious trouble."

I'd never heard Dad talk that sternly to another adult, and wasn't sure what the result would be.

"Leave right now," Dad said.

"I'll go," Blake said. "But if I have to, I'll come back. And you don't want me to come back. It won't just be talk."

And he left, slamming the door.

"Dad," I yelled, running down the stairs. "Lock that door right now."

Dad locked it, and I peeked around our front window shade.

"He's walking down the sidewalk. He's got some kind of limp. OK, now he's in his pickup."

"He looks awful," Dad said. "His face is blotchy and pimply. And he stinks."

"Was he drunk?"

"Maybe. Smells like he peed on himself."

Dad was right. The air near our front door smelled like his piss-soaked sweater.

"Dad, he's not leaving," I said, peeking out the window. "He's sitting in his pickup."

I saw his face blaze into sight—he'd lit a cigarette. Then it was dark in the pickup again.

My heart was racing. I was convinced that Del's dad was loading a gun and in a minute would jump out and start shooting, cigarette dangling from his lips. That's the kind of thing the crazy Blake family did. They liked weapons and owned lots of them. Then I saw the headlights turn on, and the pickup lurch from the curb.

"He's leaving," I said. "He's driving away."

"I feel sorry for him," Dad said next.

"What? Sorry?"

"Yes, sorry. I feel sorry for that man."

"He said he'd kill you if you ever called the police again. So you feel sorry for a guy who might kill you?"

"He didn't say 'kill.'"

"But he was thinking it."

"Fulton Blake is a sad case. A broken man. And the things that broke him, you and I can't begin to understand. We've been lucky— even with our bad luck we've been far luckier than the Blakes."

I'd had it with Dad's sympathy popping up at the wrong time. I said a curt goodnight, then trudged up the stairs to my room. I opened my math book, decided I wasn't in the mood for problem-solving, and changed into a T-shirt and boxers I picked up off the floor. But there was no way I'd be able to sleep. If Del's dad was so angry, what about Del? What would Del do to me tomorrow at school? How could I hide from him all day, or all week, or all month? He wouldn't be Del if he didn't get revenge. Then there was a rumble of thunder—I guess the storm clouds I noticed at Jamie's house didn't just blow away. A minute later the first spray of rain hit the window.

I shifted the Medal of Honor box from under my pillow into my backpack and opened Grandpa's diary. Since there's no way I could sleep, I started to read.

8

War Diary

THE BLACK LEATHER BINDING of Grandpa's diary was battered and brittle. He'd printed his name in blue ink on the first page: Justin James Lyle. Under that, in small lettering, all in caps, "WAR DIARY." It didn't seem like the handwriting of a grown man, though he was twenty-seven when he started it. Most entries were in smudged pencil; a few in ink: I guess he used whatever he could get hold of to write. He'd mention big events with a couple words; but a whole page could be about a church steeple in some bombed-out Belgian village. Something that I might want to know about, like what it's like to ride in a half track, Grandpa would mention in passing—it was noisy, stuffy, cramped. He skipped weeks and months; 1943 was completely missing. The entry for D-Day had two words alone on a page: *Omaha Beach*. On September 4, 1944 he wrote three pages in neat handwriting about maggots crawling in the belly of a horse in a field. *I can't figure what killed it*, Grandpa wrote at the end of the third page. *No wound. Big belly. Can't figure.*

I thumbed to what most interested me: when Grandpa earned his Medal of Honor at the Battle of the Bulge. The first entry on it was December 16, 1944: *Ardennes. Artillery. No birds for 3 days.* My heart was beating at the next entry, because it was about what he'd done to earn the medal. I expected pages of description, the details I could only imagine when recreating the battle with toy soldiers. But all it said was, *December 18, heavy artillery. Dragged bodies for two hours.* He had no idea that he'd done something heroic.

The next page read, *St. Vith. Frost bite.*

January 15, 1944, had two words: *Fighting over.*

On May 8, 1945, he wrote *Horning found me in the canteen. Germany surrendered. Celebration tonight.*

He was sent home for a furlough, then reassigned to Berlin.

On June 16 he wrote: *Snipers. Werwolves.*

I skimmed through the Berlin entries. Grandpa was fascinated by how everything was broken: smashed bricks, concrete hunks in alleyways, twisted plumbing on walkways, holes as big as buses in streets, wrecked statues, whole city blocks without roofs, starving dogs roaming in packs, splintered chairs and busted tables in the lobbies of buildings, the stink of gasoline and burnt flesh. He walked by what was left of the Reichstag and bribed a Russian guard for a look inside. He wrote about feeding stations for starving Berliners. *Hundreds in line, waiting 12 hours, maybe longer, for thin soup and bread, holding up bowls, battered pots, scraps of paper. Most very young, or very old. Toss a butt on the ground, a half-naked kid picks it up.*

June 19, 1945: *Boy hung by the neck off the Unter den Linden. Werwolves?*

June 20, 1945: *Kids, barefoot, kicking a ball. The tallest saw me watching and knocked down a smaller kid just so I'd see him do it.*

July 21, 1945: *Letter from Laura: she's pregnant after the furlough. If boy, Matthew, for Laura's Dad.*

August 1, 1945: *Signed on for another stint. Wonder what Laura will say.*

Grandpa wrote about contraband and the black market.

Tiergarten used to be a park. Now, all trees chopped for firewood. You can get anything there. Liquor. Soap, coffee, candy. The Russians want watches and cameras.

On September 8, he wrote, *Jones fired up. Talking crazy.*

There was one more entry, September 9, 1945, two days before he got shot.

Last night, to the Tiergarten to deal with Ollie and Albert, see what Gerhardt has to sell. Then Chip and Andy. Heard a voice from a doorway. Girl, maybe fifteen. Followed her to a second floor apartment. In the living room: old man in an overstuffed chair split open along one arm. Pasty face, unshaved, circles under his eyes.

Girl pulled me past him to a small bedroom, oil lamp on the floor. Sat on a mattress, no sheets. I gave five dollars. She took off her sweater. I looked around: peeling wallpaper, shade drawn over a window, chest of drawers. On top of the chest, a bowl of dried flowers, a candle. Next to that: a photograph of a man in German uniform by the wheel of a bomber. "Bruder," she said. "Er ist tot," which means "he's dead." In the light of the nearby lamp, she reminded me of Laura, but thinner.

I left a pack of cigarettes.

Empty space, and these words: *You can have anything you want.*

——————

When I woke in the middle of the night, I didn't know where I was. I felt scared. Grandpa's diary was on my chest. I knew I wouldn't be taking it to school. The first chance I'd get, I'd put it back in Dad's drawer under the letters. I wouldn't tell Dad I'd read it. I'd forget it ever existed.

9

Wednesday

"YOU'RE DOING THAT PRESENTATION for history today, right?" Dad said as he flipped pancakes on the griddle.

"Yeah," I said.

"So it's a big day."

"Right."

"Did you sleep after last night's surprise?"

"I slept OK." I sure wasn't telling him I'd spent half the night reading a diary I'd stolen from his room and wasn't supposed to know about.

"Don't worry about Fulton Blake," Dad said. "He's an old-fashioned farmer. And not well socialized. And on hard times."

"Not being socialized isn't the problem, Dad. He's a psycho. Like his son."

"Justin, think about this. It's been just him and his son in that old farmhouse since his wife passed away. Imagine how cold and empty that place must be in February. I'm guessing they don't pick up after themselves much." Dad smiled. "You think Fulton Blake ever tells *his* son to clean up his bedroom?"

It came to me then: Dad's thinking about Mom being gone. That's where all this sympathy for Fulton Blake comes from. He's thinking about a man and his son living alone.

"And don't forget the business on the other side of that family, what Frank Herd did to his wife. It's all terribly sad." Dad shook his head. "Anyway I'm glad you got some sleep. Remember what I used to do when you were a baby and couldn't sleep?"

"I don't remember much about when I was little."

"I'd carry you to the living room and put on John Hiatt's 'Lipstick Sunset.' And we'd slow-dance until your eyes finally shut. It was the only thing that worked."

"Slow-dance?" I said. "Please, Dad. We never slow-danced."

He laughed, and moved to other subjects: his grocery list, a drippy bathroom faucet, next week's union vote at the college. Most everything went in one ear and whooshed out the other because the only thing on my mind was this: if Fulton Blake was so angry at Dad, imagine how angry Del will be at me.

I stood and slung my backpack over a shoulder. "I'll see if Danh's ready to go."

The truth was, I wanted to find Danh because I was afraid to bike to school by myself. I was terrified of Del's car sneaking up from behind, cutting me off, Del and Tommy charging out, knocking me down and doing God knows what to me. I knew Del would think I'd ratted on him. He'd blame me for whatever his crazy father did to him as punishment. That's how things happened with guys like Del: when they got hurt, they only blamed someone they could hurt back. I wheeled my bike from the garage, leaned it against the railing by our front steps, and sat down. It couldn't have rained too much last night because the ground looked damp, not soaked. My eyes drifted to Danh's house, then to our Honda Civic in the driveway. The car looked different—smaller or, it turned out, lower. I ran into the house.

I found Dad shaving in the bathroom.

"Someone slashed our tires," I told him.

"What?"

"Every tire's flat, with big gashes all over."

"Blake," he said with disgust. "It's got to be. Unbelievable."

He splashed water over his face and, barefoot in his khakis and white T-shirt, walked outside and around the car.

"Fulton Blake is dumb as a brick," he said. "They don't come any dumber."

The sad case, I thought. The broken man. The not well socialized person, right Dad? But what I said was: "Don't call the police. We don't know for sure it was him."

"Of course it's him. He drove a block away, parked, dug out a hunting knife, and walked back to slash those tires. If he'd just punctured them, they could be patched. But he's made them unusable. He knew exactly what he was doing. Replacing those tires will cost five hundred at least. There's no way I'll get the money out of Blake."

"Hey, Just!" a happy voice shouted.

It was Danh, wheeling his bike towards us, big smile on his face. Then he stopped. "What happened to your car?"

"Let's go or we'll be late," I said. "I'll tell you on the way. Bye, Dad."

But Dad didn't hear me. He was on his knees on the driveway, inspecting the damage.

———

As we biked, I decided it wouldn't help matters to tell Danh the truth about the car. The less said about the whole mess, the better. Then maybe it would settle down, just fade away. So I told Danh that Dad had driven over roofing nails at a construction site near the college. I worried that Danh had seen that the tires were slashed, but he didn't say anything. Then he told me that he'd spent last night researching the Medal of Honor on the web. I was glad to get on a different subject.

"Guess what I found out," he said.

"What?"

"There's a lot of fake heroes around."

"Yeah?"

"Hundreds. There's stores where you can buy silver stars, bronze stars, medals of honor. So these guys buy them, then pretend to be someone they're not. They join parades on Veteran's Day. They give speeches about all the fake heroic things they did. But there's this guy Mitchell Paige who spends his life tracking down the fake heroes. Fake heroes make him crazy. He found one who's a judge in Illinois, and nailed him for. . . ."

I didn't want to hear about pathetic people pretending to be heroes. I let Danh just talk so I could keep lookout for Del. Danh must have realized I wasn't listening, because he stopped biking in the middle of a sentence when we reached the Jordan house.

"Let's check out the cat family."

"No time," I said. "And besides, it's boring."

"There's lots of time, see." He held up his wrist, showing a brand new watch. "We've got twenty-one minutes."

"Where'd you get the watch?"

"A birthday present."

"When was your birthday?"

"Yesterday."

"Christ, Danh. Why didn't you tell me?"

"Well," he said. He looked around, everywhere but at me. "I don't know."

"Did you do anything special?"

"Mom baked a cake. Dad said we should invite you over, but you'd just been over, and I knew you were at Jamie's anyway, so I said you were busy."

"OK," I said. "OK. Next year I'll come over for your birthday."

Then we saw the mother cat bound out of the hedge and race towards the porch.

"Hey," Danh shouted, "she's carrying another kitten."

The cat stopped in her tracks and we got a good look. She wasn't carrying a kitten. She was carrying a chipmunk missing its head.

"God," Danh said. "That's disgusting."

"Let's go," I said. "Right now, or we'll be late."

"She's taking care of herself and her family," I said next, since Danh seemed pretty grossed out by what he saw. "She's doing what she has to do"—which made me think of Fulton Blake. Was he doing what he had to do, no matter how bizarre it seemed to anyone else? Maybe he was no worse than a mother cat with a headless chipmunk between her teeth.

———

We biked without talking. Danh was probably thinking about the chipmunk, but now I was going over what happened during my dinner at Jamie's.

"Danh," I said. "Ever hear of a chess player named Vladimir Kramlick?"

"Kramnik," Danh said. "He's OK, but Kasparov's the best. After Kasparov, Bobby Fischer."

Kramnik, Kasparov, Fischer. Now if Jamie's father asked about chess, I'd have something to say, though I couldn't imagine sitting through another dinner with that messed-up family.

The open road felt like the most dangerous place to be, so I was relieved when we locked our bikes in the rack by the school's front entrance and headed inside. In classrooms at least there were teachers—a degree of protection, even if they were clueless about what really goes on in hallways, classes, and especially bathrooms. I didn't drink water all morning so I wouldn't have to use a bathroom. Mr. Delilah gave me a lecture for not having done the math homework—but homework, or being lectured for not doing it, was dead last on my list of what to worry about. In

German before lunch I had to pee so badly I thought I'd explode. When class let out, I ran into the bathroom at the end of the second floor. It was empty, so I could use the end stall—the only one with a lock that worked.

I heard someone open the door and walk in. My heart started thumping like a fist on a door. Whoever it was didn't use a urinal. He was quiet. I knew he was looking for me.

"Justin?"

When I opened the stall door a crack, I saw Rusty Taylor bent low, peeking under my stall door.

"Jesus, Rusty," I said. "You scared me."

"I saw you run down the hall and in here. I need to ask you something."

I walked to a sink, irritated, and turned on the faucet. "What?"

For a few seconds he examined the skuzzy, cracked tile work on the floor. Then he came out with it.

"I was thinking about, you know, Jamie Peterson. And then I was thinking, you know, about the math homework that you got in trouble for not doing."

"Yeah?"

"I had the same problem. I couldn't figure it out."

"It wasn't that I couldn't figure it out," I said, even more irritated. "I didn't have the time. I've got lots on my mind these days."

We both got quiet then.

"Rusty," I said. "What's going on?"

"I thought we could work together. On math."

"On math?" As I dried my hands with a paper towel, I felt bad for Rusty, who was the worst in class at trigonometry. Whenever Mr. Delilah scanned the class to ask someone a question, Rusty's face got this tight, desperate look, and he'd slump lower in his chair, chin to his chest—which might be exactly why Delilah liked calling on him.

"Sure," I said. "We could. Not this week though. This week's . . ." and I thought about what word to use. "This week's crazy."

"No problem," he said. "But how about this. How about we include Jamie Peterson in a study group?"

"What do you mean?"

"The three of us could study together. You know, during lunchtime. As soon as your history presentation's done."

"She's in the advanced class, which doesn't get the same assignments as us," I said. "It doesn't make sense."

"Sure it makes sense. She's smart. We can help each other. Just ask, OK?" He fidgeted with his wristwatch then blurted out, "I mean, she's hot, you know? She's really hot. What's wrong with asking?"

I took a good look at Rusty. He was still a dork, but he'd gotten tall, as tall as me. And I realized that Jamie would probably like him just fine in a study group because he's a nice guy, and honest, and a good friend.

"OK," I said. "Whatever. I'll ask."

"Great!" he said. "And don't forget about Saturday, OK? Come over around eleven."

Isn't it weird, I thought to myself, how no one sees Danh, but everyone sees Jamie?

———

When I entered the cafeteria for lunch, Jamie and Danh were at our old table, eating sandwiches and sipping milk as if nothing was wrong with the world. Tommy DeSantis, Vera Knight, and Will Hayes sat at their usual table, but without Del. Vera sat by herself at one end, staring into space, with no one talking to her, or even seeming to notice she was there. She didn't have a plate, tray, or lunch bag: her half-eaten white bread sandwich just sat on the table. Her greasy black hair hung to her shoulders, looking like it hadn't been washed or brushed in days. If she wore black eye makeup and pierced her lips and cheeks, you'd think she was goth—even East Liberty had a few of those. But she was just a plain-looking, hunched-over girl with no makeup, dressed in blue jeans, T-shirts, flannel shirts—nothing fancy, nothing that stood out. She was quiet, spookily quiet. No one could figure what she saw in Del, or Del in her—not that anyone spent much time trying to figure Vera out. Suddenly she turned around, catching my eye, and I walked quickly to where Jamie and Danh were sitting.

I took a huge breath, and exhaled every scrap of air in my lungs because of this amazing realization: Del wasn't in the cafeteria. He was absent from lunch. That certainly meant he was absent from school. Now I could use bathrooms. Now I didn't need to check over my shoulder every ten seconds. Now I could breathe.

"Did you bring it?" Jamie asked when I sat down.

I'd been so preoccupied with seeing Del, or Del seeing me, that I'd forgotten about the medal. I nodded.

"Can we have a look?"

I took out the little wood box from my backpack. "Listen," I said to Danh. "Don't make a big deal of it in here, OK?"

Danh shrugged, a *Me? Me make a big deal?* kind of shrug.

"Let's see it," Jamie said.

I opened the box and we checked out the ribbon, the eagle, the star, the little goddess of war.

"It's smaller than I thought," Jamie said. Then, embarrassed, she added, "But it's really beautiful."

———

Del was also absent from history, my last class of the day. He's not here! He's really not here! I got through the day! I screamed the words in my head while Mr. Horn finished taking roll. I can't remember ever feeling so relieved, which might be why Jamie and I gave a good presentation. Jamie profiled medal winners, including Mary Edwards Walker, a Civil War surgeon and the only woman to get a medal. I ended my part with an account of what my grandfather did during the Battle of the Bulge—I was careful not to brag—then passed around the medal in its box. Of course Tommy DeSantis stuck in a big finger when the box came to him. He even leaned over to smell it. No wonder the guy failed two grades, I said to myself.

During question time, a girl asked if anyone had won a medal for fighting in Iraq. "Yes," I said. "A guy named Paul Smith."

"What's he do now?"

"I don't know. He's dead." I didn't intend what I'd said to be funny but kids laughed. I felt sorry for Paul Smith.

Danh asked if anyone ever faked getting a Medal of Honor.

"Yes," I said. "Hundreds. They buy them, then wear them in parades, pretending to be heroes. But someone named Mitchell Paige spends his life tracking them down." Danh nodded happily.

There was a sour note when Chip Sorrelli, a smart aleck, said, "Isn't there a problem with that Bob Kerrey Vietnam Medal?"

"We're not going there," Mr. Horn interjected. "Your question is off topic. This is a presentation on the Medal of Honor, not a debate about Senator Kerrey."

From the back row Tommy DeSantis raised his hand, which surprised everyone, since he never asked questions.

"Yes?" Mr. Horn said.

"So that thing's valuable, right? I mean, you can sell it for money?"

"It's valuable to my dad," I said.

"Worth a lot?"

"I don't know. Maybe if you put it on eBay."

"Where do you keep it?"

"In a safe deposit box."

"Tommy," Jamie said. "Where would *you* keep a Medal of Honor?"

"Me?"

"Yes, you. Assuming you could ever be awarded one?"

A ripple of laughter moved through the room.

"I don't know," Tommy said. "Some place that's safe."

"Glad to hear that," Jamie said.

Now laughter was class-wide. Tommy kept his eyes focused on the floor, his face flushed a light pink. I wished Jamie hadn't said those things, but I knew she'd said them for my sake. She was taking care of me.

When we finished Mr. Horn smiled and nodded. "Great work, both of you. Justin, your grandfather was a brave soldier. I'm sure you're proud."

I saw that Tommy was staring at his hands, clenched together on his writing desk.

"I think that went well," Jamie said as we walked out, closely followed by Danh.

"Yeah," I said. "We did OK."

"OK?" Danh said. "Just OK? That was amazing. I bet you guys get an A."

"Horn doesn't give many A's," Jamie said, "but maybe."

And we were quiet then, standing in a little circle outside the classroom door.

Say something, I told myself. Say the next thing. What's the next thing to say?

"OK," Jamie said, starting down the hall. "See you later."

"See you," I called out.

"See you," Danh said, in echo mode.

And I stood there next to Danh, disappointed. I'm not sure exactly why. I'm not sure what more I expected.

―――――――

After history I went to my locker for my backpack. As I spun the combination dial I sensed someone behind me and turned to see Vera Knight, her dull brown eyes that didn't blink.

"Jesus," I said. "You scared me." And I thought: you float around this school like a ghost.

"I wanna tell you something," she said.

"OK."

"It's a message."

"From Del?"

"From me."

That was a surprise. "All right," I said.

"You better be careful."

She said this and everything else in the same monotone, as if one word had no more meaning than the next.

"That's the message?"

She nodded. "Because someone's taking an interest."

"In me?"

She nodded again.

"What's he going to do?"

"What's he *not* going to do?" she said, and her lips formed a strange little smile though her eyes weren't smiling at all. "That's the question. That's always the question."

"I've gotta go," I said. "I'm meeting a friend."

She took hold of my hand. "You're not like my brother," she said. I could feel the hard scabs on her palm from when she fell in front of my house. Her grip was surprisingly strong.

"Excuse me?"

"Hugh's got rough hands, like Del. You've got soft hands."

I jerked my hand out of hers, grabbed my backpack, shut the locker, and walked away as quick as I could. When I turned down the hall leading to Danh's locker, I started running, dodging kids who were talking or holding hands or just milling around. I was out of breath by the time I reached Danh, who was kneeling on the floor, sorting through books.

"Vera Knight just talked to me," I said.

"Who?"

"Del Blake's girlfriend. She never talks to anyone. She appeared out of the air next to my locker. Just now she probably said the most words ever in her life, to anybody. And it's me she said them to. She's completely weird. It's like she doesn't have a personality. I hope to Christ she doesn't follow me."

"Nobody's following you," Danh said, peering around me. He stood. "What'd she say?"

"Only weird stuff. Something about her brother—I didn't know she had a brother. And that I need to watch out. I just want to stay away from her."

"Stay away from her and from Del," Danh said. "That's my advice."

"Can you finish with those books?" I said. "I really want to get going."

"What's the rush?" He shut his locker and slung his backpack over a shoulder.

"I'm sick of school," I said. "I need to get moving."

"Yeah," he said. "I know what you mean."

"Let's bike home by a new route, what d'ya say?"

I figured the most dangerous part of the day would be the ride home, when Del might be roaming around, searching for me.

Danh looked at me strangely, but nodded.

"Just follow me," I said.

———

"You sure you know where we're going?" Danh asked after we'd biked for twenty minutes. "This isn't what I'd call a scenic route."

"Don't worry," I said. "It's not far now."

I was leading us on a complicated loop down side streets rarely visited, with little ramshackle houses crowded together. I'd lived in East Liberty my whole life, so I had a general sense of how to get around. Newcomer Danh had to follow my lead. Lots of houses we passed had "For Sale" signs hammered into the fenced-in, overgrown front yards. One time a huge German Shepherd that must have been lying in wait for kids on bikes barreled out of nowhere, barking and growling until he hit the chain link fence, when he leaped and tried to scramble over the top. He almost made it too. I thought I saw foam spilling out of his mouth.

"Wait a minute," Danh called to me, slowing after we'd raced far enough ahead of the dog. "I've got no idea where we are. If we take too long, my mom will worry."

"I know exactly where we are," I said. "It's another ten minutes, that's all. You don't get around East Liberty much, do you?"

"Not much."

Then we saw a car turn onto the street, moving slowly, which made my heart skip—but I relaxed when I saw it wasn't Del's Grand Prix but a white Toyota Corolla with rust spots all over. A second later I almost fell off my bike when I recognized Tommy's face over the steering wheel, and next to him Will Hayes's block-shaped head. And alone in the back seat, Vera's small, dark head, barely visible. The car swerved in front of us, and Tommy and Will jumped out. A cigarette dangled from Will's lips.

"Well I'll be damned," Tommy said, a big grin on his face. "At long last. We wondered where the hell you'd gotten to. We almost gave up. Now get off the bike."

I did like he said.

"The slanty-eyed kid can leave."

Danh turned to me, terrified.

"Go home," I said. "It's OK."

He put a foot on a pedal but didn't start up.

"That way," I said to Danh, pointing straight ahead. "And then the first left. Go on a little and you'll see where you are. Really, you should go. Right now." And he took off.

"We want to show you something special," Tommy said when Danh was out of earshot. "Just for you. We keep it in the back seat. Come on over."

But I wasn't going in that car.

"Move," Will said, "or we drag you. Which would be fun, right Tommy?" He flicked his cigarette to the sidewalk. "That'd be OK by me."

Will Hayes was one of those football players on the verge of being fat: not fat yet, but ninety-nine percent there. Because he had to move all those pounds around on the football field, he'd developed muscles. If he had any memory of the night when he dared me to cross the imaginary line he drew on the dance floor, he didn't show it.

What was in the back seat? A blindfold and handcuffs? A bucket of piss to pour over my head? I walked over slowly, my mind racing with possibilities. When Tommy opened the car door, Del Blake rose up from a crouch in the back like a vampire from a casket, grinning, his upper lip so swollen it seemed about to pop. Both eyes were puffy, ringed with dark purple bruises. He wore a frayed jean jacket but his left arm was in a sling that looked like it'd been torn from a dirty sheet. Vera sat as far away from Del as she could, pressed against the driver side door.

"My God," I said to Del. "What happened? Are you OK?"

"You think I look beat up?" he said. "Find a mirror in an hour. We'll be twins."

As he spoke, I noticed that a second front tooth was now missing.

"I didn't do anything. My dad saw your license plate. Dad told Boland to check it out."

"You're blaming your old man?" he said. "That's pathetic. That's as low as it gets. Even I haven't done that."

"No, I'm telling the truth. He phoned Boland about what happened. I never told anyone anything."

"Don't bullshit me. You told him you saw me driving. It's all over your face. Funny thing is, this came out of nothing, didn't it? I've done a lot worse than make Tommy dump piss on someone. I've hurt certain people real bad. That cup of piss was less than nothing. But it's started now, hasn't it? And once a thing like this starts up, there's no stopping it. Now it's got an ugly life of its own."

"It wasn't my fault," I said. "I didn't want you to get hurt."

"Hurt?" Del said. "You have no idea about hurt. Nobody does but me. I've had an education in it from day one. I got a certificate in hurt. But I'll get even. I don't know how yet, but I'll do it. Bugsy got his, didn't he? Did you know it was me who let Bugsy off his chain? I knew he'd bolt for the Jones farm. Knew he'd get into that chicken coop—sniffing all that shit in the air was driving him nuts."

"Your dog?" I said. "The one that got shot?"

"That thing bit me for the last time. And soon Pop's gonna get his. That's a hard one, but it's gonna happen. He'll get his own education. He'll find out a few things about *hurt*." He smiled. "And maybe you will too."

Then something in Del's face changed. "Get in," he said. "You and me, we're gonna finally have a heart-to-heart."

I took off my backpack and slid next to him because I didn't have a choice. Tommy shut the car door, and he and Will stood in front of it, so I couldn't jump out. Vera was still pressed against her door, staring ahead at the windshield, as if sleeping with her eyes open. I could feel Del's eyes on me. No one said anything. I kept my focus on the dirty floor, where I saw a glass tube with a bulbous knob at one end: a pipe. And next to it, half hid under the front seat, a furry gray tail. A real tail. I turned to look out the greasy window at Tommy and Will.

"See something?" Del said.

"That tail," I said. "A squirrel's tail."

"Never seen one before?"

"It's not attached to anything."

"My God," Del said, "you are one fucking observant guy. How'd you learn to see so much?"

Del couldn't know, but I was remembering the dead squirrel I saw on last Sunday's walk with my dad. A squirrel without a tail.

"Look at me," Del said. "Look right at me. Right now."

I faced him, and swallowed hard.

"You think you've got it rough, don't you? That getting through life is a hard slog."

"What d'you mean?"

"You think you've got it rough because you look like a jackass and no one pays you attention. Am I right?"

Tommy and Will both snickered, but stopped short when Del snarled, "Shut the fuck up you two. This isn't funny. This jackass here, he's a lot more like me than either of you. And maybe I'd be more like him if I hadn't been born into a goddamned torture chamber. There's more in his head than in your heads put together."

He turned back to me. "So, be honest, is life rough for you? Do you feel sorry for yourself?"

"Sometimes," I said.

"Sometimes. Like for example, you're sorry for yourself because your mom started fucking some guy and left you with your dad in this shit-hole town."

I felt my throat tighten as he talked.

"Yeah, I know about all that. I made it my business to find out about you and your nothing family. I'm paying you some attention now. You think you've been on a devil's roller coaster because your baby brother got all the attention. First it was just you. Then it was you and him, wasn't it? What did you use? A pillow? Your hands? My guess is a pillow—no marks that way. And anyways, you were just trying to make him comfortable, right? Wasn't your fault. You were just a kid. It's the lack of air that killed him."

"I didn't do anything like that."

"No, of course not. You're just like me. I never did anything my whole life. But now I'm gonna do something. Now I'm going to be your teacher, and you'll learn a lot more from me than in that shit history class. Let me tell you something: all that you think is crap in your life is nothing. You're on easy street. You'll always be on easy street. I could knock two teeth out of your mouth so you'd look like me, and you'd still be on easy street. I could break your arm and you'd go home to live on easy street. You'll never have to fight for what you need, but you don't have a clue about that, do you?"

"Maybe not," I said.

"Give me your wallet."

I just stared at Del.

"Give me your wallet," Del said again, "before I loosen up those teeth of yours." He smiled. "Don't feel bad. This is part of your education."

I handed it over, and he took out my money.

"Pathetic," he shouted to Tommy and Will. "Two dollars. Who carries two dollars in a wallet?" He turned back to me. "I don't need your two lousy dollars, but since they're yours, I'll take them. That's how much you mean to me." He tossed me the wallet and gave the money to Vera, who stuffed the bills in her jeans pocket. "Now get that thing out of your backpack."

"What thing?"

"That thing you passed around in Mr. Jew-Boy's class. The medal Tommy saw. Don't play dumb."

With a shaky hand, I unzipped the backpack and handed Del the box.

"So this is what gets my bitch cousin so wet?" With his good hand, Del hung the medal around his neck. "I guess I'm the big hero now, right? Because if you've got a medal, you gotta be a hero. Go ahead, say it. Say 'you're the big fucking hero now.'"

"You're the big hero now," I said quietly.

"Hey," Tommy said to me through the still open car door. "Bet you wish you'd left that in the safe deposit box, huh?"

"This thing isn't any big deal," Del said, running a thumb over the face of the medal. "Maybe I'll keep it, maybe I'll toss it in the garbage. Or pawn it for a couple bucks. Or give it to Vera. Would you like that, V? Would this thing make a good birthday present? It's the thought that counts, right?"

Vera shrugged.

"How's your dad gonna feel when you don't bring it home? Will he be disappointed? Ask a couple of questions? Then maybe break your arm? Throw you around the kitchen? Yank out a perfectly good tooth with some pliers? Hit you in the face with a whiskey bottle? Tie you to a chair for half the night and stub out cigarettes on your chest?"

I saw Tommy and Will glance at each other nervously as Del said that last part.

Del leaned close to me, to see if his words were having an effect. They were. I was churning up inside. My hands, jammed in my pockets, shook like an old man's.

"Hey," Del said. "I've got something to show you. You'll like this." He reached into his jean jacket pocket and took out his tobacco tin—the same that he'd shown me on the bus back when we were friends, with "B. F. Gravely" embossed on it.

"I remember that," I said.

"I don't think so," Del said.

"Your good luck charm."

"Right," Del said. "You guessed it. A charm. That's the word. Charm. For good luck."

"You showed it to me once," I said. "On the school bus."

"Nah," he said. "I didn't."

He opened the lid. Inside wasn't chewing tobacco but hair. A coil of jet black hair, tied in the middle with dirty-looking brown twine. The hair was attached to a little piece of what looked like leather.

"Grandpa Herd brought it back from Vietnam. Cut it off a gook's head. A gook about sixteen, he told me, maybe younger. I stole it from Gramps when he went to prison. It's kind of like a medal, right? A good luck charm medal that no one knows about except me and you. And Vera. But V knows how to keep a secret."

The weird thing is that he wasn't smiling when he said all that. He was serious. For him it really was a kind of medal.

"Got a great idea," he said next, setting the tin on the seat. He took the Medal of Honor off his neck and set it in the tin on top of the coil of hair. "Don't you think they belong together? Don't you think that now I'll get all the good luck in the world?"

"Sure," I said.

"Can't miss," Del said.

I nodded.

"Bullshit," he said.

I stared at the squirrel's tail on the car floor. Poor, dead squirrel, I thought.

"I've changed my mind," Del announced, shutting the tin's lid and slipping it in his jacket pocket. "I think you're OK. I'm not gonna fuck you up. You're like a brother to me—a long lost twin brother. Why should I do the usual thing? Instead, we'll take a ride, a nice relaxing ride in the country, how's that sound? We'll be a couple of brothers taking a ride."

I nodded.

"Just like the old days you think you remember but that never happened, right?"

I nodded again.

"We'll leave the squirrels alone, OK? Don't you worry about them. They'll keep their damn tails."

"OK."

"Great. I'll show you what I do for my brother. We'll have fun. We'll have a smoke, how about that?"

"No thanks," I said.

"No thanks? That's funny. That's a riot. You don't know a thing, my friend. You're gonna try some weed, and you're gonna try something better than weed. Something I save for special friends, because it's too special for just anyone. So you're gonna try, and you're gonna succeed. It'll change your life. You'll be a superman, a jackass loser superman. If you don't try, we go back to Plan A, and just fuck you up. But Plan B is better. In Plan B maybe Vera can show you something she's got. Some icing on the cake. Would you like that, V? Show our new friend a thing or two, that nice icing you've got? Here's an interesting girl," Del continued. "Nobody sees her, right? Nobody but me. But there's more going on in this fucked-up head than you could imagine. Maybe she's quiet, but there's more churning around in this one than in any bitch in the whole school, even that crazy cousin of mine. You don't know the half of it, what that girl put up with before I got to her." He reached with his good arm and unbuttoned Vera's flannel shirt to the middle so I could see her dingy white bra. Will Hayes turned to have a look too. All the while she kept staring ahead into space.

"She's sweet on you, that's what I think," Del said. "But here's the thing. Maybe see a doctor after. Better safe than sorry, know what I mean?"

"Can I just go home?" I blurted out.

"Don't worry, you'll be home for dinner. You'll be in kick-ass shape for dinner."

I looked down. A long rip ran across the upholstery between us, as clean as if someone had sliced through with a knife. I had to try something, and only one idea came to me.

"Remember when we took the bus?" I said. "I was on the bus that picked you up. We used to sit together."

Del shook his head as if he felt sorry for me.

"We talked about books," I said. "And other stuff."

"You don't know me," Del said.

"You read science fiction," I said.

"Let me explain something." Del spoke slowly and deliberately. "I never read a book in my life. I'm not like you. In fact, I'm not like anyone you know. And the reason is, when I get a beating I can't remember anything before that beating. So I've never seen you before today. It's all blank. All gone. And do you have any idea how many beatings I've had in my life?"

"No."

"It's amazing I remember my name," he said, and laughed, a nasal cackle, like nothing I'd heard before. "It's amazing I remember how to piss in a toilet. It's amazing I remember not to slit my own throat with Gramps' knife."

I glanced anxiously out my window, where Tommy and Will stood guard. Then I felt a spasm down low, and something warm on my leg. It took a second to realize I'd pissed myself.

Del wrinkled his nose then started shouting, "Get the fuck out of this car! Get the fuck out! Christ, the stupid shit pissed his pants." He was howling with laughter. "You're a fucking child."

Tommy opened the door, and I grabbed my backpack and stumbled out. Tommy and Will took hold of my arms.

Then we saw a police car with lights flashing turn the corner and rush in behind Tommy's car. Tommy and Will let go of me, and I saw Del duck down out of sight. Vera buttoned up her shirt as Jack Boland jumped out of his car and walked quickly towards us.

"You OK, son?" he asked me.

I swallowed hard. "I'm OK."

"What're these boys doing?"

I shrugged.

"Did they hurt you?"

"No."

"I was just apologizing," Del shouted from inside the car.

Boland turned to him. "Get out."

Del slowly stepped out, his good arm pressed against his chest—I could tell he wasn't faking the pain. Boland looked him over, from his beaten-up face to his broken arm to his hurt ribs.

"Apologizing? Really? Justin, is that true?"

I hesitated. "Yes sir," I said. "It's true."

"Pops told me to apologize. Said he'd break my other arm if I didn't." And Del started softly laughing.

Jack Boland shook his head. I guess that seemed like something Fulton Blake would actually say to his son.

"You got alcohol in that car?"

"No, sir," Del said.

"Drugs?"

"No. We don't mess with that stuff."

"Mind if I have a look?"

"Go ahead. But I'm not sure you're exactly allowed to search the car. I mean, it belongs to Tommy's dad, and Tommy's got a regular license. You're older than all of us, right Tom? Not that failing was your fault. With Tommy, teachers only see the rough, not the diamond inside. Anyway Officer, when you got here the car was parked, wasn't it? Legally parked. It's not like you saw Tommy speeding or driving crazy or anything."

"Don't be a smart ass," Boland said, his voice low and threatening. "You don't want to be a smart ass with me."

He opened the front passenger door, peered around, then opened a back door and did the same. Boland didn't say a word to Vera, who sat perfectly still, arms folded over her chest. I was sure he'd find the glass tube on the floor, but Del must have stashed that before he got out. And I guess Del or Vera had pushed that squirrel tail deep under the seat. The last thing Boland did was open and shut the trunk.

"All right," he said. "Why don't you boys drive someplace where you won't get into more trouble? Home might be a good idea."

"Will do, sir," Del said. "Home is always great. Just love to be home. How about you," he said to me. "Need a lift back to that great family of yours? I'm sure Tommy would oblige, him being legal to drive and everything."

I shook my head no. "Got my bike."

"OK," Del said. "Suit yourself."

Tommy and Will jumped in the front seats, Del eased himself into the back. As Tommy pulled away from the curb, I could see Vera's pale oval face staring at me through the rear window, her fingers on the top button of her shirt.

I shouldered my backpack.

"What were they really up to?" Boland asked me. He gestured at the wet streak down my pants. "Looks like you had an accident."

Now it wasn't just my hands shaking: it was my entire body, but I managed to get words out. "Del wanted to apologize. That's the truth. But, you know, the guy scares me. That's what happened. I got scared."

"Delroy Blake is a bad kid," Boland said. "A really bad kid. Did you see anything? Alcohol? Drugs? Paraphernalia? Now's the time to tell me."

"I want to go home," I said. "Can I?"

Boland nodded. "You can go home. But you should give me something. It's important. Tell me what really happened."

"I told you. Del wanted to apologize."

"All right," Boland said. "But do me a favor and talk to your dad about this. I'm telling you, those kids are capable of anything."

"OK."

"Why don't I drive you home? Then I can have a word with your dad."

"I'd rather bike," I said.

And I picked up my bike and started towards home, knowing that Jack Boland's eyes were on me. I biked without thinking, without looking back to where I'd been, or forward to where I was going.

Somehow I got to my house, went directly to my room, and crawled into bed. With the covers over me, I started crying, using a pillow as my Kleenex, then as a punching bag. I was crying because I'd let Del have the medal without a fight. I was punching because I felt angry: at Del and Tommy, but also at my dad. My stomach started aching then because what happened made me think about Grandpa and the girl in Berlin, the dead brother in the German uniform, and the old man in the chair—his pasty face, the circles under his eyes. Strange how things that seem so random can connect up in your head, whether you want them to or not.

———

Just before dinnertime the phone rang. Dad yelled up that it was Danh.

"Did they beat you up? What happened? How'd you get home?" Danh asked as soon as I said "hello."

"I didn't get beat up."

"You didn't? That's great. I thought for sure you would. I couldn't figure out where I was, and made some wrong turns, so it took me a while to get home. I phoned the police as soon as I could. But I didn't know exactly which street you were on."

"Boland got there after Del took the medal."

"Del took your medal? Didn't Officer Boland make him give it back?"

"I didn't tell Boland about it."

"Why not?"

"Because then Del would do something worse to me tomorrow." I hated myself for sounding like such a coward. "That's how it works. It never stops. One bad thing leads to something worse. Boland couldn't protect me."

"You told your dad what happened, right?"

"No."

"Jesus, what're you going to do?" Danh seemed about to burst into tears. "You've got to do something."

"I don't know. I'll eat dinner, I'll watch TV, then I'll go to bed and pretend to sleep. I'll wait till this week gets over."

———

At dinner Dad had his own bad news to tell, but didn't come out with it until we were washing dishes.

"You should know something, Just. Something about the college."

"What?"

"They're getting rid of my position."

"What position?"

"My teaching position."

"Your job?"

"That's right. My job."

"I thought you had tenure. I thought they couldn't fire you."

"If they get rid of your position, they can fire you without firing you. It'll take a while, but that's their plan."

"That's not fair," I said. "That's a loophole."

"Enrollment's down, so they have a case. At least that's what they're saying. But the real reason is that they don't like the work I'm doing for the union. And I'm fifty-eight. They want to replace me with someone younger and cheaper."

"What'll you do?"

"I'll fight. The union will fight with me. And we'll see what happens."

I thought Dad might give more details, but he just kept on wiping the last pots silently, mechanically with a sopping wet dishtowel, so they were more wet at the end than when he started. What did he want me to say? I couldn't help him. I had problems of my own. So I said, "That really sucks," and we finished the dishes without talking—he didn't even tell me not to say "sucks."

10

Thursday

I TOSSED AND TURNED most of the night, trying not to think about everything churning in my brain. I felt terrible in the morning, with a thumping headache, and told Dad I was too sick to go to school, but he put a palm on my forehead and said my temperature was normal.

"You don't always have symptoms when you're sick," I said.

"You don't seem yourself, that's true," Dad said. "But your temperature's normal and you're not throwing up, so you'll have to go to school."

"I need to see a doctor."

"No you don't. I'm not canceling classes to take you to the doctor because you feel out of sorts."

"'Out of sorts' in most people's vocabulary means sick. Go teach your classes. I'll be fine at home."

"You're going to school, and that's final. Get ready."

Dad was out of sorts himself, which I guess losing your job will do to you. He had on his frustrated, distracted look. When I was maybe five or six and Dad got frustrated with me, he'd put that look on and ask a string of questions, as if the questions themselves would make me behave better. Are *you* the be all and end all? The epicenter of the known universe? The king of all you survey? The entity in existence that most matters, is that what you are? Though I didn't know what "epicenter" or "entity" meant, or the difference between the known universe and any other, I could easily answer his questions: Yes. Yes. Yes. I am. What else would I be?

Danh and I biked to school in silence, side by side. I could tell he was dying to say something about Del taking Grandpa's medal and me not telling the police, but he held it in. We were both too nervous about keeping an eye out for Del's Grand Prix or Tommy's rusted Toyota to risk talking.

I dragged myself through my morning classes: social studies, math, gym, study hall, German. I passed Jamie in the hall once, and she flashed a big smile, and I smiled back—a fake smile, a liar's smile. I deserved the bad things that were coming my way. When Jamie found out who I really was, she wouldn't smile at me any more. On the way to the cafeteria after German, I wondered if our lunches together would continue now that we'd given our presentation. I had the answer as soon as I walked in: Jamie was eating at a different table with three girlfriends. One, Kirsten Hanley, was talking loudly. "Becky's going to have to get used to it, that's all," she was saying. "It's over. He's mine now and there's nothing she can do about it." As far as I could tell, Jamie didn't see me.

Tommy DeSantis, Vera Knight, and their friends were at their usual table—everyone except Del and Will Hayes. Danh sat by himself at our old table. He waved, and I started towards him, the bag lunch my dad made in my hand, but Tommy got up and intercepted me. I must have looked scared because the first thing Tommy said was, "Hold on. Relax. You're safe. We're in the cafeteria. I just need to tell you something."

I located the teacher on duty, old Mrs. Hendricks, leaning on her cane, chatting with one of the cooks. I knew that if Tommy started trouble she'd be absolutely no help.

"What is it?" I said.

He glanced over his shoulder then half whispered, "I feel bad about what happened yesterday."

I thought he must be joking, but he wasn't. "You feel bad?"

"Yeah, about Del taking that medal thing. I didn't know he'd actually keep it." He scanned the cafeteria. "Sorry for pushing you around. Did it for Del. Not my choice."

"OK," I said. "It's OK." I was ready to sprint out the door at any sudden movement.

"We need to talk," he said. "Just for a minute. Let's go to the hall."

"Why the hall?"

"I don't want anyone seeing us."

But I wasn't budging. The hall wouldn't even have useless old Mrs. Hendricks for protection.

"I've got an idea," he said. "I can help you get that medal back."

"What do you mean?"

"The thing Del took. I can help get it back."

"Why?"

He hesitated. "To repay you. You know, for not turning me in like you did Del."

"I didn't turn Del in."

"Boland knows Del drove the car, but he doesn't know I tossed the piss. You did me a favor."

"I didn't tell anyone anything."

"There's another reason we need to talk. So come on, follow me."

I walked behind him through the door to the empty hall.

"What's the other reason?" I said as soon as he stopped.

"You can't tell anyone, not even the gook you hang out with. Swear you won't tell anyone."

"I swear."

"It's Will." Tommy's voice dropped to a low whisper even though we were alone. "He's all messed up."

"What do you mean?"

"Del messed him up."

"Why?"

"I'm not sure. No one's talking. Something to do with Vera. We were at Hopkins Park last night, a bunch of us. You know, partying at one of those picnic areas. I guess Will stepped over the line with Vera. I didn't see anything, but something happened." Tommy let out a soft laugh. "The thing is, with Del, you never know where the line is. Damn thing keeps moving. And Vera, well she's a whole different story. Del takes care of her. You know, in his own way. Anyway, he's gone."

"Del's gone?" This was the first hopeful thing I'd heard.

"No, you idiot, Will. Will's gone."

"Gone where?"

"Don't know. I was pissing in the woods and heard this loud shout. I ran back, and there was Del up close to Will with this huge army knife stuck in Will's mouth, actually *inside* his mouth—the same knife his grandpa stabbed his grandmother with. I wonder if his gramma's blood ever got cleaned off. But isn't that wild? Del's all banged up with an arm in a sling and he can still get a knife into a guy's mouth who's twice his size. Five or six guys are standing around, staring. Vera's there too, just staring. Will's mouthing something no one can understand, probably 'I'm really sorry' or 'would you take that knife out of my mouth?' But Del's not listening. He's saying over and over in this weird voice, 'You want to fuck with me you fuck?' He's saying that to Will like it makes sense. Then he puts his lips next to Will's ear and whispers. No one knows what. Only Will knows. And Del. When he's done whispering, he takes the knife out of Will's mouth, and tells me to drive Will home, so now I've got to leave the party, though at this point it's not much of a party. All the way home I'm trying to get Will to tell me what Del said, but he won't. His eyes are shut tight like he can't stand to see anything. I swear his knees are shaking. I tell him I'll pick him up for school the next morning and he nods, OK. But in the morning, no one answers the door at Will's house. The car's gone, and all the shades are down."

"Maybe they took a family trip."

Tommy laughed out loud. "The Hayes family? Their only trips are to the liquor store or the Indian casino on weekends. No, they got Will out of East Liberty for his own good. Whatever Del said to Will, it must have been bad. Beyond bad. I've had enough of that guy. You know? The way things are going, someone's gonna get terminally messed up. And that someone could be me."

He glanced up and down the empty hall. "But if I help you get the medal back, you need to help me. It don't come free. I scratch your back, you scratch mine."

This was baffling. What would Tommy need? Help cheating on an exam? Plagiarizing a paper?

Mr. Garvey, the principal, appeared at the other end of the hall, walking towards us with a clipboard in one hand.

"Come on," Tommy said, "let's go back in the cafeteria."

I followed him through the door.

"Jamie Peterson," he said, turning to me.

"What about Jamie?"

"I've asked her out lots of times but she always says no. She's definitely not seeing anyone. She's not a lez. No way. Too hot to be a lez."

"I can't help you with Jamie," I said.

"She eats lunch with you," Tommy said. "See, she's waiting."

It was true. She'd left her friends and moved to sit with Danh at our old table. They were both fixated on me and Tommy.

"I heard that she's not, you know, involved with you. Is that right?"

"Yeah," I said. "That's right."

"I know that kiss-ass Marty Tower's been sniffing around her for a month with no luck."

"I think so."

"OK." Tommy was satisfied. "Then I need to make a move. Put in a good word for me. Soften her up. Tell her I'm not like

Del. That guy's out of his fucking mind. I mean, I like a little fun as much as the next guy, but he's a total freak." Tommy thumped my back as if we were now friends. "Tell her I'm helping you out with Del. Tell her I'm OK. She sees us right now, being friendly. Almost buddies. Work on that, OK? Then I'll ask her out to a movie or a party. I need to hook up with that girl. I'm crazy about her. She's total class."

Thoughts raced through my head: Does Tommy really want to date Jamie after how she humiliated him in history? Does Tommy even understand what she did? Is he stupid? Or is he smarter than anyone thinks?

"How do I get my medal from Del?"

"You know where the Blake place is, on Bishop Road?"

"Yeah."

"There's an old barn behind the house. Del fixed up a room in there for a hangout. His old man doesn't care what we do. He's drunk in his living room easy chair most of the time anyway. So Del and me dragged in a couch, some chairs and stuff, a table. Del hung your medal on a nail behind the couch. I saw it last night before we went to the park. Get inside that barn and you can't miss it."

Why is he telling me this? I thought. What's going on?

"Here's the thing. Del's taking the week off from school because of how his dad beat him up. Can you believe he's got cracked ribs? And that thing about cigarette burns on his chest, that's true. He showed me. He says that's the least bad thing his dad did to him. But he'll keep on partying. That guy never stops. So Friday night Del and me and the guys are heading to the barbecue pit at Hopkins Park. We'll drink, hang out. We'll be there by eight. Del's old man gets shit-faced at the Old Shoe every Friday night. Goes for happy hour and doesn't leave till it closes. He doesn't get happy, just completely fucking shit-faced, according to Del, then passes out in front of the TV. Ever notice he's got a gimp leg? Del says he tried to get up the stairs drunk one time, fell all the way down, and hasn't walked right since. Anyway, the guy never misses the Old Shoe on a Friday night. So just get to that barn and take your medal. No one'll be there. It's easy."

"I'm not an idiot, Tommy," I said.

"This isn't a double cross, promise. This is real. I'm sick of Del's craziness. That guy's gone way beyond crazy. But he'll definitely be at that Hopkins Park party. You just get to the barn by eight-thirty and you'll never see Del or his old man."

"If you really want to help me, why don't *you* get the medal?"

"I need to be around Del when it goes missing so he won't think it's me who took it. And I can make sure he stays at the party real late. I'm your insurance. That's my end of the deal."

"Why wouldn't he guess it was me that took the medal?"

"He thinks you're chicken-shit, a nobody. To Del, you're a . . . you're a bug crawling around on some shit. The last thing he'd believe is that you've got the balls to go to his hangout and take the medal back. He'll think his dad found it, then got drunk and forgot about it."

"Del threatened me in his car. Would he do that if he thinks I'm nobody? He said he's paying attention to me now."

"Just talk," Tommy said. "Del talk. You're not the first. Won't be the last either. He enjoys freaking people out. Lives for it. Wants to make you piss your pants. Oh shit," he added. "Didn't mean that last part."

"No one will be in the house or the barn?"

"Definitely no one," Tommy said. "Del doesn't have anyone except his old man. In his family, people have a way of getting killed, or put in prison, or going crazy—their brains aren't the same as ours. Del painted 'Keep Out' on the door you should use. Not the big double doors, but the regular door with a lock on it. The key's under a flat rock next to that door. Easy as pie. But remember, I need that date with Jamie after you get your medal.

I need to see more of her, know what I mean? That's your end of the deal, OK?"

I stared at him for a few seconds. "OK," I said—simple enough to say, but what I promised wasn't simple at all.

Marko Wolf walked up just then and stopped in front of Tommy. A short, skinny kid with a blond crew cut who was always sucking up to Del, his eyes were shiny, as if someone had brushed shellac over them.

"Where were you this morning?" he asked Tommy. "I waited for a half hour by the bus garage."

"Couldn't get there," Tommy said.

"So you've got it, right? Tell me you've got it."

"I don't have it."

"What do you mean? What happened?"

"I don't have it," Tommy said. "That's what happened."

"You asshole," Marko said, punching out the syllables. "What am I supposed to tell Bets? That's the whole reason she's seeing me tonight. I'll look like a jackass."

"So you look like a jackass," Tommy said. "You look like what you look like—why should I care? You'll get it tomorrow. Now move away. Can't you see I'm busy?"

Marko turned to me for the first time. He looked at Tommy, then back at me.

"What's the point?" he said.

"The point is," Tommy said, "that you need to leave. You'll get your shit tomorrow."

Marko stared at me for a few seconds, blinking his eyes. Then he saw my bag lunch.

"Is that mine?

"No," I said. "It's my lunch."

"Lunch? What do you mean?"

"My lunch. Sandwiches. It's lunch time and we're in the cafeteria."

"Oh yeah?" Marko said, as if he didn't believe a word I'd said. "Is that right?" He glanced quickly back at Tommy.

"Yeah, that's right," Tommy said.

Then Marko slowly walked away.

"He gets messed up every morning," Tommy said to me. "Oh yeah, one more thing. Sorry about that business with your dad and the piss."

"Why'd you do that anyway?" I said. "Because of our 'No Bush No War' election sign?"

"What?" Tommy thought for a second. "Nah, nothing like that. And it wasn't my piss. Belonged to Will. There's something scrambled in that guy's head too, you know? Nothing to do with me. Someone said 'toss the piss.' Vera maybe. I think it was Vera brought up the idea. Then Del got hold of it, and made me do it. You know, the way Del makes you do things. But it was Will's piss. I swear to God it was his and not mine."

"Why would Vera think that up?"

"Who knows why anything gets into her head? Why does anyone do anything anyway?"

Tommy put out his hand, and I shook it. It felt dry as sandpaper.

———

After I set my bag lunch on our table, the first thing Jamie said was, "I can't believe those jerks took your medal."

I shot Danh an angry look that made his eyes pop out.

"Don't blame Danh," Jamie said. "I knew something was bothering you, so I made him tell. What's the point of keeping it secret? You need to talk to your friends more. And you need to talk to your dad about what happened. You keep too much inside."

"I can't tell my dad. He doesn't even know I brought it to school."

"He doesn't?"

"No."

"Well, now you've got to tell him."

"I'm not telling him."

"Why not?"

"Because then he'll know I lied, and won't trust me again. And I don't want him involved. He's got enough on his mind."

"What's on his mind?" Danh asked.

I looked from him to Jamie.

"He might lose his job."

"I thought college teachers were, like, immune from getting fired," Danh said.

"He's not getting fired," I said, sharply. "More like laid off."

I felt my eyes watering, which Jamie might have seen because she kept her eyes on the table until I swallowed hard and got control.

"At the college?" Danh said.

"I guess they can't just fire him. But he's definitely worried."

"Listen," Jamie said. "One day your father will want to show the medal to someone, and it'll be gone, and he'll ask you about it. You'll have to explain what happened sometime, so why not now?"

"He doesn't show it to anyone," I said, "and I'm not telling him I took it."

"What will you do?" Danh asked.

"Maybe I can get it back."

I told them what Tommy had said about the medal hanging on a nail in Blake's barn, and that I should go and get it Friday evening when the house would be empty.

"That's what you two were talking about?"

I nodded.

She thought for a second. "That's good information. But this is real fishy. Why would Tommy want to help you? What does *he* get out of it?"

"He's sick of Del, I guess. And scared of him too. Tommy didn't seem so bad just now. I believe him when he says he's sorry for what he did."

"Not so bad?" Jamie laughed. "Sorry for what he did? He's a complete sleaze. I know girls he's dated, and the date's always about fighting him off." She looked thoughtful. "Why'd you shake his hand?"

"Because he told me where the medal is," I said, not looking Jamie in the eye but hoping she'd believe me. I took a sandwich from my lunch bag and examined it: ham and cheese. I slid it back in.

"Don't trust him," Danh put in, "or Del. They're up to something."

"It's true those guys hang out at Hopkins Park on Friday nights," Jamie said. "Marty told me that. Marty goes there some-times, but he's not like them."

"How do we know that Del will really be at the park?" I said. "Just because Tommy says so doesn't mean anything."

"I've got an idea," Jamie said. "I'll ask Marty if he's going on Friday. I'll say a friend of mine needs to know if Del's there. I'll call Marty on my cell, and if he says Del's *not* there, we'll know it's a set-up."

"We can meet behind the Jordan house with our bikes and flashlights," Danh said. "Then we'll bike together to the Blake place."

"Wait," I said. "You guys can't come. It might be dangerous."

"Dangerous?" Danh said.

"We think we know what's happening, but we really don't. And even if Del is at Hopkins Park, we can't be positive his dad will be at the Old Shoe. What if this Friday is his one exception? Maybe he'll get sick and won't go out."

"Yeah," Danh said. "Maybe we shouldn't do this."

"Justin needs to get the medal back," Jamie said. "And I'm definitely going along."

"I'm going too," Danh said.

The truth is, I wasn't brave like my Grandpa. I don't think I could have gone by myself. But I knew it wasn't right for my friends to put themselves in danger.

"Here's what we'll do," I said. "We meet behind the Jordan house. We bike to the Blake barn together and Jamie calls Marty to see if Del and Tommy are at the park. And if they're at the park and no one's in the house, I'll go in the barn by myself. If I don't come straight out with the medal, Jamie calls my dad on her cell. OK?"

"OK," Danh said.

Jamie nodded.

So there we were, the three of us. Jamie looking serious and determined. Danh looking more than a little scared. And me—I was feeling pretty good. *I'm not alone!* I said to myself. *These two are with me.*

———

History, our last class, was a joke. Tommy and Marko were supposed to present on German U-boats. But all they did was pass around Nazi stuff supposedly from World War II but definitely fake: armbands, an iron cross made of aluminum, a swastika pin, massive belt buckles that bikers around East Liberty like to wear, propaganda posters, even a folded Nazi flag that felt like the plastic cover for a picnic table. Marko did most of the talking—an incoherent ramble about the eagle and the swastika as ancient symbols of power. His eyes were as glassy as in the cafeteria. At the end Tommy brought out a replica of a German grenade that looked like an oil can with a handle, a gun that they called a Walther P38, and a knife. When the P38 reached me, I saw it was plastic, just a big toy. But the knife was heavy and scary-looking, the only real thing in the entire presentation. Tommy and Marko wanted everyone in class to vote on which was their favorite weapon, but Mr. Horn said that a vote on weapons was "off topic." When the knife reached him, Mr. Horn checked it over carefully. "This is US army issue," he said. "An M7 bayonet. It's got nothing to do with the German Army or the Second World War."

"It belongs to a friend of mine," Tommy said. "My friend's grandfather used it in Vietnam."

"Then it's irrelevant, isn't it? Vietnam wasn't World War II. I should know. And you should know too."

When Mr. Horn asked them to name the sources for their presentation, Marko passed around pamphlets from the American Nazi party.

"OK," Mr. Horn said. "This has gone on long enough. Sit down, the both of you."

The bell rang, but Mr. Horn made everyone stay put. "Before you go," he said, his voice tight and high pitched, "I want to say something. This presentation was lazy and uninformed. It's supposed to be about submarine warfare during World War II, not a bunch of paranoid fantasies. 'Stupid' is too kind a word for what we listened to. It's sick. It's just sick. You both act as if death isn't real. You can take it from me that it is."

I'd never seen Mr. Horn so upset. His hands were shaking.

As they packed up their notes and the weapons, Tommy looked happy enough—like he hadn't understood anything Mr. Horn had said. But Marko was pissed off.

"You're prejudiced," Marko said, loud enough for the class to hear.

"What did you say?" Mr. Horn stood from his chair.

"You're prejudiced. That's why you didn't like our presentation."

"Prejudiced against what?"

"Against people who think different."

"You're right," Mr. Horn said. "I am. I'm prejudiced against stupidity. I'm prejudiced against moral sickness. I'm prejudiced against kids who love guns and knives out of ignorance and bad parenting and idiotic ideas about what can make them feel important."

Mr. Horn closed his eyes for a few seconds. He knew he'd gone too far, but couldn't bring himself to backtrack, or apologize.

"I don't want to see those trashy flyers in this school again," he said. "Now please, all of you, get out of this room."

———

Vera was waiting for me in front of my locker, hands in her pockets, shoulders hunched as usual. She looked like she expected someone to slap her head at any second. I thought about just walking past, but she could be crazy enough to stand there forever, and at some point I needed to get my stuff.

"You're standing in front of my locker," I said.

"I know," she said.

"Can you please move?"

She shifted over enough for me to open the lock. I was so nervous with Vera standing there just staring, it took three tries to get the combination right. I squatted and pulled out my backpack and a few books and notebooks. I wasn't going to say anything. If Vera had some new message, she could just come out with it.

"I'm not what you think I am," she said. "I'm not what anyone thinks."

She waited for a response, but I busied myself with stuffing books into my backpack. Then I stood.

"OK. What are you?"

"A person."

"I know that." I shut my locker and spun the dial.

"Then how come you don't see me?"

"I do. I see you now."

She stared directly into my eyes. Then she squinted, as if trying to bring me into focus.

"No. You don't. You're lying."

"I saw you in front of my house on Sunday," I said. "I tried to help you. But you didn't want help."

She reached out to touch my arm but I pulled away.

"Why?" she said.

"I'm sorry," I said. "I don't know what you want. I don't know what to do."

"You don't know because you're an asshole," she said, and swatted the back of my hand, digging in fingernails that left four parallel scratches.

"Jesus!" I yelled, yanking my hand away. "What's the matter with you?"

"See me now?" she said calmly, a twisted smile on her lips. "See what I can do?"

"You're a psycho," I said. "You're exactly what everyone thinks you are. You just wish you weren't."

Instantly I wanted to take back those words.

"You're not different," she said, backing away but keeping her eyes on mine. "I thought you might be, but you're not. You're the same. Everybody's the same, and you're like everybody."

And she turned and walked away.

————

Danh and I biked home at top speed without talking. Everything was just buzzing through my head as I biked. What was going on with Vera? Was Tommy being honest? Why did I agree to help get him a date with Jamie? Why did I have to lie to Jamie?

And now I knew something I didn't want to know, that Del had a knife, and was happy to use that knife—it had to be the one his grandfather used to stab his already dead grandmother. The houses and street signs passed by as if I was biking in a dream. As we reached my house, I asked Danh to stop for a minute.

"I feel like I might throw up," I said.

"What's wrong? Are you sick?"

"I've got to tell you something."

"What?"

"Tommy DeSantis wants me to do a favor in exchange for his help getting the medal back."

The rising nausea fell away.

"A favor? What favor?"

"Get him a date with Jamie."

"He likes Jamie?"

"I guess."

"Well, she *is* the prettiest girl in school. But she doesn't like him. In fact, she can't stand him. She can't stand him because he's . . . well, he's the second scariest person in school. And Tommy's completely different from Jamie in every way you can think of. It'd be like two different species trying to . . . you know, get together. It'd be like a normal nice person and a screwed up alien . . ."

"Stop," I said. "I know. I'm aware of that."

"And you told him you'd get him a date?"

"I had to. I mean it happened so fast. All of a sudden I was shaking his hand on a deal that I'd thought about for ten seconds. No, not even that long. I didn't think. You get swept up, you know? Like . . ." and I surprised myself with what I said next. "Like my grandfather."

"What do you mean?"

"I don't mean anything," I said. "I don't know what I mean."

"What will you do about Jamie and Tommy?"

"Nothing. At least for now. What *can* I do? After I get the medal back I'll figure out what to do."

"Shouldn't you tell Jamie?"

"It's too late," I said. "Definitely too late. And you can't tell her anything about this. Promise?"

"Yeah," Danh said. "I promise."

———

An open can of Delmonico's Beef Stew sat on the kitchen stove next to a pot. I ate it cold in front of an old *Growing Pains* episode about Mike being at a party when someone was passing around cocaine.

When the kitchen phone rang, I waited until the fifth ring.

"How are you doing?" Jamie asked.

"I'm OK."

"I've been worried about you."

"I'm all right. A little stressed."

"Tomorrow will be fine. It's an adventure. Think of it that way. We're doing something exciting together." She sounded almost cheerful. "Marty says the party's on for tomorrow at the park, and he's going. He's expecting me to call about whether or not Del is there. So we're all set."

Then we talked for a while about ordinary things: how I hated basketball, how her girlfriends at school were forever talking about shopping or boys or their weight. When I asked how things were going with her family, she said, "Dad's always on edge. Tony talks constantly about going back to Brooklyn Heights, where he says he can have some kind of a life, but Dad says there's no way we're doing that. Mom cooks and cleans like a robot even though Mrs. Braddock cleans the house every Saturday morning. The good thing is, they pretty much leave me alone."

"I wish my dad would leave me alone," I said. "But there's no one else he can bother." For some reason that made Jamie laugh.

"Danh might call you tonight," she said. "I asked him to check in. He's such a sweetheart, the little brother I never had."

And that, of course, made me think about little Mike. Maybe if he'd grown up, he'd have been like Danh—good-hearted and smart and loyal. The little brother you always wanted.

———

For the first time in my life a girl had phoned me to talk. Just to talk. I felt like I'd entered a new dimension of life. When the phone rang a minute later, I ran to pick up, thinking it could be Jamie again, or maybe Danh.

"Justin."

It was Mom. Thursday night—how could I have forgotten the Thursday night call?

"I tried earlier, but the phone was busy."

"A friend," I said.

We started off as usual, each trying to get the other to talk.

"How was your week?" she asked.

"Fine, how was yours?"

"Good, real good. But tell me what's going on. What'd you do today?"

"Nothing much. It went by fast."

"OK," she said. "So tell me about your history presentation."

"It went fine. Mr. Horn liked it."

"And the medal? Did your father let you take it to school?"

I swallowed hard. "No."

"I'm not surprised. He would never put it on display at home, like people do with family heirlooms. Never showed it to anyone that I can remember. That medal is complicated for your father. It was the same for your grandmother—she never liked talking about that medal or the war. You'd think your father would be proud of it, but . . . he keeps it hidden, doesn't he? I guess he's the one who'll have to tell you why it's a problem."

We were quiet for a few seconds.

"OK," she said. "Anything else going on?"

"I found something yesterday."

"What's that?"

"Grandpa's diary."

"His war diary?"

"Yes."

"Your father let you read it?"

"I found it by accident. I guess I should have told Dad. Why didn't he ever mention it?"

"His idea was that you could read it when you're old enough."

"I'm fifteen."

"I know, but a few parts might be hard to understand. Your grandfather did an amazing thing to earn that medal. An astonishing thing. We can all be proud of that. But he wasn't perfect. From what your father and your grandmother told me, he wasn't perfect.

"Are you all right?" Mom asked when I didn't respond.

"I'm a little sick."

"What's wrong?"

"The flu."

"And your father let you to go school?"

"I don't have a temperature."

"Did he call a doctor?"

"No, Mom, really, I'm fine. Something's going around. It's no big deal. How about you? Did you catch it?"

Of course she couldn't have gotten "it" since "it" didn't exist, and even if it did, the "it" was in East Liberty, not San Diego.

Mom's answer to my question was totally unconnected: "I want to come home."

"Come home? To East Liberty? I told you Mom, I'm not that sick."

"No, come home to stay." Then she added, "It's not working with Gerald. I'm trying as hard as I can, but it's not working out."

I didn't know what to say. Of course I wanted her home. It's the one thing I've wanted since the day she left. It's the thing I prayed for even when I wasn't sure I believed in God. Of course I missed her, and loved her. I hated Gerald and his family. Hated the ways he tried to get me to like him. Hated San Diego. Hated that my family wasn't a family. Hated the phone calls, because phone calls meant she couldn't be here. But is it ever possible to come back? Could Dad forget all that had happened? Could I forget?

"Why don't you tell Dad?" I said.

"I'm not saying I want to be with your father. I just want to come home."

"You don't want to be with Dad, but you want to come home?"
She didn't respond.

"Say that again. Because I can't believe what I heard."
Again, silence.

Then something in me snapped. Words started gushing in my head. First she falls in love with her professor, then out of love and in love with her boss. Now it's out of love again and . . . and what? I could feel something boiling deep inside, and that boiling turning to anger, rising from the pit of my stomach through my throat to my face. I was angry for Dad, angry for me, plain angry. Then words started flowing out.

"You're supposed to be my mother," I said, "not just yourself. Not just yourself in some bubble. Can't you be a mother?"

"I'm trying to be," she said.

"You're not trying hard enough. Not near. Does every other word have to be 'me' or stupid 'Gerald'? You don't have any idea what you did to us, do you? Or else you know and don't care. Every night I see Dad moping around our house because you're not here. He still loves you. Do you think he can cook anything decent? He tries, but he can't. His fish stinks. His pork chops are like rocks from the garden. Everything sucks. You're three thousand miles away cooking for people I don't even know, thinking a couple of phone calls a week will make everything OK. Well, they don't. They just don't. Everything is definitely not OK."

I'd never said anything remotely like that to my mother—or to anyone. I wasn't sure where all that stuff about food came from. But I did know that I'd taken a step over a line—a line I hadn't realized I was anywhere near. And there was no stepping back and pretending it didn't happen. I'd walked into a new world, an alien world in which you could say any bad thing you wanted—and anyone could say anything they wanted back. Because I'd gotten myself in that place with Mom, I felt like there were no boundaries anywhere, at all, ever. So I braced myself for my mother's onslaught—a litany of all my faults, all the ways I was a crap son, everything she could never normally say because of the line she wouldn't go over before this phone call. Now she could, because I had. And it would hurt.

Then I heard a strange noise. It took a second to realize that my mother was crying. Then she spoke.

"I shouldn't have said anything. It's hard to know how much to say to you. I don't feel . . . I don't feel like myself. I don't know how to be myself."

Then my anger melted away. Somehow without trying I'd jumped back into the normal world. The world that made sense. Mom didn't want to be angry. I didn't want to be angry. I just wanted Mom to be Mom.

"I don't know how to be myself either," I said. "Not really."

"You've got a good heart, Justin. That's who you are."

"Thanks Mom," I said. But this was all getting to be too much. So I added, quietly, "Got to go. Homework and stuff."

"OK," she said. "But I want you to know something."

"What?"

"That I understand how much I hurt you by leaving. Few things can hurt more than a mother leaving. I couldn't say this until now—not even to myself."

"It did take a while," I said. "Not that I've been waiting."

Then she surprised me—she laughed a little, and her laughing made me realize I'd made a joke.

"You *have* been waiting," she said. "I've been waiting. What took so long?"

———

I know what I felt when Mom moved out of the house, but it's hard to imagine what Dad went through. I never had a girlfriend. I never kissed a girl. Lots of other guys my age have girlfriends. Some are having sex, or at least say they are. They have fights and break-ups. There's generally three relationship dramas happening in the cafeteria any given day, someone sulking, someone crying, someone ignoring someone who's sitting right next to them. But one thing I can't imagine is what it's like to get married, then find out your wife is seeing someone else without you having a clue. And this thing I can't imagine is exactly what happened to Dad.

The phone rang again, but I didn't answer. It might have been Danh. But it might have been my mother calling back to talk some more, and cry some more. It kept ringing. Why couldn't Dad just buy a stupid answering machine? Nine rings. Ten rings. I couldn't take the pressure.

"Hello?"

"Hello. Am I speaking to Justin?"

"Yes."

"This is Reverend Haroldson. Is your answering machine broken?"

"We don't have one."

She laughed. "Well, your father needs to move into the twenty-first century. But that's part of his charm, isn't it?"

I had nothing to say to that.

"Is he in?"

"He's teaching."

"Would you tell him Betty Haroldson phoned? About dinner on Saturday. Just to confirm."

"Sure."

"You won't forget?"

"I won't forget."

"And how are you? How's school?"

Was I supposed to say that everything's fine, except that I might get stabbed by a psychopath, or killed in a worse way by his more psychopathic father?

"Fine," I said. "I'm fine, and school's fine."

"That's just great." I could tell she was thinking about what to say next.

"Remember, these are the best years of your life," is what she came out with.

I kept quiet.

"Give my best to your father."

"I will."

"Goodbye Justin."

"Goodbye."

I made a mental note: Dad's Christmas present this year would be an answering machine, no matter what he says.

———

A program on the war in Iraq was on TV. Seventy-five Americans killed during August, the highest count all year. It's funny that you never hear about heroes in Iraq, only casualties. And you never see the bodies. I heard there's a law against photographing the bodies. Five years ago if anyone asked who my hero was, I would have said Dad, because that's what any ten-year-old would say. Now that I'm fifteen, what would I say? The president? He's a joke. The generals who lead the war in Iraq? I don't remember their names. There's no living person I would call a hero.

11

Friday

WALKING DOWN THE SCHOOL HALLWAYS and sitting in classes felt unreal, like walking up that stairway in my dream about Tijuana.

Jamie, Danh, and I were co-conspirators, possessors of a secret no one else who saw us knew, or could imagine. It was exciting and strange to feel so separate and so together. The hands on the school clocks ticked away minutes and hours. They seemed slowed down, though of course each minute was the same length as yesterday's, the same as the day before, and the day before that. Students and teachers walked back and forth in the halls, talking, thinking thoughts about their own lives, having nothing to do with us.

During third period gym we divided into teams for basketball, and I played weirdly well in those slowed-down seconds and minutes. When I dribbled, no one could catch me, block me, or steal the ball. I'd stop and shoot, and the ball would arc through the basket with hardly a swish. I wasn't myself—I was someone who could play a sport. It had to do with my mind being elsewhere, so my body could function without my head. My body liked that arrangement. The coach whacked me on the back as I jogged by after a three pointer, giving his patronizing "nice shot, son, we'll make a ball player out of you yet." But towards the end of the period, my mind and body renewed their relationship, remembering the old days, and the coordination broke down. Before the bell rang the coach yelled out: "Lyle, play some freaking basketball! Pay some attention! You should have blocked Williams! What the heck happened?"

Jamie, Danh and I sat together for lunch but didn't talk about Del or the Blake farm or the medal, or what was ahead of us. We talked about everyday things, things you wouldn't remember the next day. Danh had finally started relaxing around Jamie—stopped the apologizing, the staring, the long silences. Tommy was in the cafeteria, holding forth for the same friends who used to cluster around Del. He'd taken over Del's role as leader of the school's tough guys, as if Del wasn't gone for a few days but gone forever. The one time I caught his eye, he winked, but kept on talking.

If Del wasn't in school, I thought, where was he? At home? That was hard to believe. Alone in his hangout in the barn in the dark, waiting for me, his grandpa's bayonet in his hand? Or maybe in a car driving along country roads, brooding, planning his plans.

In Mrs. McShane's seventh period English class it didn't matter that I hadn't finished *Macbeth*: she talked most of the time about a trip she took to Edinburgh when she was in college. Rusty didn't even bother to hide the *Superman* comic he was reading.

Mr. Horn didn't show up for history. Instead, we had a substitute, Mr. Johnson, who looked about a year older than us. A mustache of a dozen brown hairs curled over his lips. He dressed in wrinkled khaki pants and a tweed jacket a size too big, like something his mother bought for him. He announced that the class would become an extra free period: we could do what we wanted as long as we stayed in our chairs. Most students took out books and notebooks. Tommy slouched in his desk chair and went to sleep. I opened up *Macbeth* and tried to read from the beginning of act five, which starts with Lady Macbeth going crazy. I stopped at some lines that seemed familiar. Maybe I remembered them from a *Macbeth* performance Dad took me to in Syracuse:

Out, out, brief candle!
Life's but a walking shadow; a poor player,
That struts and frets his hour upon the stage,
And then is heard no more. It is a tale
Told by an idiot, full of sound and fury,
Signifying nothing.

Macbeth suddenly made sense to me. He was smart. He could plan. He could organize. He could stab someone. He could follow through. He was strong. He was tough. He didn't care. At the end he didn't care about anything but himself. People did what he said because they were afraid of him. Macbeth was Del's kind of hero.

When the bell rang, I walked over to Tommy, getting up from his chair.

"Del's not at school," I said. "Is he staying home today and tonight?"

Tommy was irritated—no longer in best buddy mode. "I already told you, remember? He's taking the week off from school. But he'll be at the park tonight. Definitely not at home tonight. You're not wimping out, are you? You're not that bug Del thinks you are, right? You're going to the barn like we planned."

"Maybe," I said, to keep Tommy off guard. "I'm not sure," and before he could say anything I rushed out to the hall where Danh was waiting.

"Come with me," I said, "right now," and I pulled him along by his arm.

"Where?"

"To my locker."

"Why?"

"Just come, OK?"

I didn't want to say, "I need to get away from Tommy and I'm afraid that twisted girl Vera might be waiting for me again."

Vera wasn't waiting. But my locker was wide open, all my books and notebooks strewn over the hall, some with pages ripped out and bunched into tight little balls. Dripping down the inside of the locker door was a long slick of spit. I unraveled one paper ball—a page from my history book about the Great Depression.

"What's going on?" Danh asked. "Did Del do this? How'd he get in your locker?"

"Vera," I said. "It could only be Vera. She watched me open the lock yesterday and must have seen the combination. She's mad at me, but I have no idea why. Jesus, this is too bizarre. I've got Vera's spit in my locker. Help me clean up and let's bike home fast."

———

"Just," Danh said as we unlocked the bikes from the rack in the school playground, "how come you never biked to school with me before this week? Why'd it take us so long to become friends?"

"I don't know," I said. "How come you never stopped by my house before?"

"I'm shy."

"Well," I said, "I'm shy too."

"I'm shyer," Danh said, and smiled. One of those quiet jokes that he recently started telling, or that I started hearing.

"Some things take time," I said. "Or luck. But it's different now. Now we're friends."

Rusty Taylor sprinted towards us across the playground.

"Did you hear about Mr. Horn?" he asked. His red cheeks were the same color as his crew-cut hair.

"He's out sick," I said. "So we had a substitute."

"He's not sick. He's in the hospital in stable condition, whatever that means. I just finished telling Jamie Peterson the story."

"What happened?"

"He got beat up last night, pretty bad. In the parking lot by his apartment. Someone heard him yelling for help and called the cops. But whoever did it got away."

"Beat up? But Horn's a big guy. And a Vietnam vet."

"He still got beat up."

"God," I said. "That's strange. Who'd want to beat up Mr. Horn?"

"Fred thinks it's Nazis. And Jamie thinks so too. You know, because of what Horn said to Tommy and Marko in class. The Nazis know he's Jewish. I guess they had ski masks over their faces."

"What Nazis?"

"Marko."

"Marko couldn't beat anyone up," I said. "Not even me."

"No," Rusty said, "but his dad could. And his dad's friends. Marko's always bragging about his dad's tough friends."

"We gotta go," I said to Rusty, since I'd heard all I wanted about fringe people in East Liberty.

———

Dad was at the kitchen table looking serious and stern when I got home.

"Everything OK?" I asked.

I was certain that Boland had talked to him about having rescued me from Del, and probably that I'd pissed my pants. Or else Dad had found out that Grandpa's medal and diary were missing from his drawer. Something bad was on his mind. I braced myself for anger, the onslaught of questions. At that moment I actually wished he *had* found out about Del and the medal, because then I'd be forced to tell everything. And he *absolutely* wouldn't let me bike to the Blake farm. He'd go himself. Or he'd call Jack Boland. He'd make sure I was safe.

"I might as well tell you," he said. "When I got home this afternoon, I found an envelope in our mail box but no stamp or return address."

"What's in it?" I said.

"Fifty dollars."

"Who'd give you that?"

"It's got to be from Bernie Schill."

"Why?"

"Jack Boland called an hour ago to tell me Bernie's in a cell at the station. He's phoning everyone Bernie robbed. The idiot was driving through town in the same pickup he used for the burglaries, same license plate, same everything—and of course got stopped for running a red light. On top of everything, he'd been drinking. Bernie told Jack he'd come back to East Liberty to give me the fifty dollars he took from our house because I'm the only one who ever treated him right. So he put that envelope in our mail box then decided to take a drunken spin around town."

"If he gave back the money, then that's good," I said. "That's good news, right?"

"I think it's good, but Jack doesn't. I didn't like his tone when he said he was keeping Bernie at the station. He's pretty angry. He wants Bernie to tell him who's dealing drugs in East Liberty." Dad shook his head. "Jack says he'll do what it takes to find out. But that's not right. The boy deserves a lawyer."

"Bernie *did* rob us," I said, to interject reality into the conversation. "And he robbed our neighbors, then ran away after you gave him a chance to make good. So he broke the law, or broke like three laws. And you also think he's on drugs, right? Shouldn't he have to tell the police what he knows?"

"Bernie's got problems. But he tried to do something good."

"Yeah," I said. "I guess."

"Jack Boland isn't above the law. I phoned him just before you came home, and he wouldn't take my call. He's a good man, but . . ." Dad stopped himself, then decided to go on, "but he's got a dark side. He sometimes thinks the end justifies the means. I don't know that he's ever bent the law much. But I wouldn't put it past him."

I wasn't sure what to think about Boland's "dark side," or how Dad might help Bernie. I had to get organized for the meeting with Jamie and Danh, so I just said the lie I had prepared—which sounded to my ears exactly like a lie I had prepared.

"Jamie wants to get together tonight to study for an exam. Is that OK?"

Dad's sternness dropped off his face. "Sure," he said. He smiled and nodded. "Of course it's OK."

"I'm supposed to be there by quarter to eight."

"That's really . . . That's wonderful."

"Yeah Dad," I said. "I know."

Dad glanced at his watch. He was forcing himself not to say more on the subject. "OK, I'll get dinner ready. And I'll do the dishes tonight." He managed a smile. "I'm glad you've got, you know, a friend to be with. It's more fun to study with a friend, isn't it?"

"Yeah," I said. "Lots more fun," and thought to myself: at least he didn't say "girlfriend."

———

Until Jamie turned on her flashlight, I didn't see either of them. She wore a black sweater, black jeans, black sneakers, everything black as night. Danh wore a brown sweater and blue jeans. I had on blue sweat pants and a dark blue sweat shirt.

"What exactly did you say to Tommy DeSantis about me?" were Jamie's first words.

It took a few seconds for her meaning to sink in.

I turned to Danh. "What did you tell her this time?" Anger churned up from my stomach. "What's the matter with you? Can't you keep anything to yourself?" And his chin sank to his chest.

"Don't blame Danh," Jamie said. "He did the right thing, unlike you. He actually talks to his friends. He can't help being honest. Just tell me what you told Tommy you'd do. Tell the truth this time."

"He said he wanted me to fix him up with you."

"Like a pimp?"

"No. He just asked, that's all."

"And you didn't tell him that he's out of his stupid mind? That nobody fixes me up with anybody?"

"No."

Jamie shook her head. "So that's why you said nice things about him yesterday. You were trying to get me to like that cretin. That's sick."

"I guess so."

"What else did you lie to me about?"

"Nothing."

"Do you really play chess?"

Danh, who'd been staring at his feet during this exchange, shot me a surprised glance.

"What do you mean?"

"When you were in the bathroom the night you had dinner at my house, I defended you. Dad said you were lying to impress me. He said you're a fake and a liar, that your dad never played chess, and that you didn't either."

"Maybe you should go home," I said to Jamie. "Maybe you shouldn't be a part of this."

"I'm in it now," Jamie said. "You and Danh don't have a cell phone, remember? It's my job to hear from Marty about whether or not Del and Tommy are at the park."

"I'm sorry, Jamie," I said. "I'm really sorry."

She pulled her cell from her pocket and speed-dialed Marty.

"Hi, it's me," she said. "I'm fine. . . . Yes, that's right. . . . Is Del there? . . . OK . . . what's he doing? . . . You're kidding me. . . . Really? . . . That's so disgusting. . . . What a pig. They're all pigs. . . . How about Tommy? . . . They are? . . . Will Hayes and Marko Wolf? Right. . . . Call me if Del leaves, OK? . . . Thanks. You're the best, Marty. I'll call you later. Bye.

"Del's at the party," Jamie said. "He's making out with his strange girlfriend, Vera what's-her-name. Tommy and his friends are there too, sitting around watching Del and that girl. *Watching* them, like they're on TV. Isn't that sick? Can you believe I'm related to that guy?" She shook her head.

"Did Marty say Will Hayes was there?"

"Yes, why?"

"I'd heard he was out of town."

"Well, he's definitely at the park with the rest of them."

What does it mean, I wondered, that Will and Del are friends again so soon?

"Do you want to do this?" Jamie said.

"OK," I said, "let's go."

———

After a quarter mile down Bishop Road the streetlights ended. It was eerie biking along an almost pitch-black road. The sky was hazy, so the sliver of a moon over the evergreens didn't give much light—just enough to see occasional bats flapping and swirling over our heads. Then a bank of clouds moved in, blotting out the moon. I'd never biked in that kind of blackness before. We rode single file in silence—me, Jamie, Danh. The only sound was the hum of our bike tires. It didn't feel real to be rolling along with only a dim awareness of trees on either side—more like rolling on air or on a black void.

I knew from the bus route years ago that Bishop Road inter-sects Stop Gap Road just before the Blake farm. From that inter-section we could see the rambling farmhouse set back from the road, one dim light in a front window, the shade drawn. We wheeled our bikes into a field a little ways from the house, set them down in the long grass, and started walking. We stopped at an apple tree by the driveway. When I looked up my eyes locked onto a hole in the bank of clouds where I could make out the big dipper—clear and bright. And seeing it up there just the way you always expected was comforting—reminding me that there are some things that don't change.

"Doesn't look like anyone's home," Danh said. "There's no car."

"I'll go by myself from here," I said, taking my flashlight out of the bike bag.

"If anything happens, or if you're not out in ten minutes, I'm calling your dad," Jamie said.

"Or 911," Danh said. He added, "You know, if it's necessary. Which of course it won't be."

"Good luck," Jamie said, and she squeezed my arm.

———

The driveway was empty. No flickering TV. Except for that faint light in the front room, the house was dark. All I could think about was how I *really* didn't want to run into Fulton Blake after seeing how he'd beaten up his own son, so I stood where I was in the dark, staring at the empty house, scanning for the slight-est movement inside. Everything was completely still. My heart was pounding like crazy, but I forced my feet to move. I walked around the house and saw the hulking side of the barn, just as Tommy had said. I wove between black shapes set here and there like scary modern sculptures: junky cars and pickups, or parts of them, up on cinder blocks. Clouds had now spread far back from the sliver of a moon, so I could see the barn clearly. It must at one time have been painted red, but in the moonlight was a weathered, muddy brown. I stood still and listened again for any person moving or talking, but heard only the wind rustling the evergreens behind me.

I saw the barn's big double doors, and around the corner, the door Tommy told me about, with the words "KEEP OUT" painted straight across in huge, white block letters shimmering in the moonlight. Underneath, in smaller letters, "CONDEMNED" and "DANGER" were scrawled. The door was padlocked just as Tommy said it would be. Now I had to use my flashlight, and shined its beam along the wispy grass. Sure enough: a large, flat stone to the left, a key underneath. I unlocked the padlock and set the key back under the stone. Then I hesitated. Had Del painted those words to keep people out? Or was the barn like half the rundown barns around East Liberty, and in the dark the rotten roof would collapse and bury me in rubble?

I stepped back, then thought about Grandpa's medal hanging on a nail behind a couch: it might actually be easy to snatch the medal, run back to Danh and Jamie, hop on our bikes, and be home in no time. If Dad was doing something downstairs, I'd sneak into his bedroom and drop the medal in the drawer under the letters. I'd be safe in my own living room watching TV by nine. What Tommy had said would likely be true, that Del would never believe I'd have the courage to sneak into his party room and take the medal. He'd blame his dad.

I opened the door, which swung smoothly and soundlessly. I froze in place, ready to bolt at the slightest sign of danger. But it was quiet inside, dead quiet. I shut the door and shined my flashlight around. Instead of a big space filled with broken-down cow stalls and rotten rafters that you'd expect, someone had built in a separate room with a false ceiling from which a bank of fluorescent lights hung. The room didn't look about to collapse, but wasn't any sort of party room like Tommy had described. For one thing, it stunk horribly, as if something big had crawled in there and died. I saw why when my flashlight lit up three deer hanging upside down from big hooks. Did hunting season open this early? Two were skinned and gutted. One was half skinned. Their eyes were still in their heads. Under the heads were three plastic buckets full of something dark—blood, I guessed. At the other end of the room on a big wooden table I could make out a hack saw, a rusty hatchet, and a half dozen different size knives. A big chest freezer stood in a corner.

I thought about trying to find the switch for the ceiling lights, but then worried that someone on the outside—Del's dad, arriving home drunk from the Old Shoe, for example—might notice all that light in his barn. So I shined my flashlight around, hunting for the couch Tommy had mentioned, without luck. Beyond the table at the far wall, I saw another door, with a big keyhole for an old fashioned key. I walked slowly towards it, bumped something, and shined my beam down on a plastic bucket filled with milky water and what at first looked like huge white and pink worms. Intestines is what they were, along with hearts and lungs and organs I couldn't name. I gagged because I'd sloshed stuff from the pan onto my sneakers. I stumbled ahead to the door. If it was locked, or didn't open into Del's hangout, I'd leave right then and tell Jamie and Danh that it was all a joke at my expense.

When I swung the door open, the inrush of air burned my nostrils—cat urine, but something from a super cat, or fifty cats pissing in unison. My eyes watered up so badly I had to wipe tears away with my sleeve. I coughed and gagged, covering my nose with a crooked elbow. I saw a table, some bottles and buckets. An electric frying pan. A tattered brown winter coat hung from a hook on the wall. On a plywood shelf: mason jars, coffee filters, half-full soda bottles and jugs, plastic tubing, a red metal tank of Coleman fuel. Leaning in one corner: a shotgun.

It was the dirtiest, messiest, smelliest kitchen you could imagine. You'd want to starve before you ate anything cooked in there. The fumes made my nostrils sting like someone had shoved lit matches up them.

I walked slowly through the kitchen, careful not to touch anything or kick anything on the floor, until I reached the door at the opposite end, which opened into the main part of the original barn. I closed the door behind me because of the kitchen's terrible stink. It was a relief to be out of those cramped little rooms and into the barn itself, which smelled of animals and hay, like a barn ought to smell—a good mustiness. Again I had to wipe tears from my eyes. With my flashlight I lit up high rafters, cow stalls, heaps of old hay bales, metal buckets, and thick-coiled ropes. It was an ordinary, falling-apart barn. There wasn't a kids' hangout in sight. The only rooms in this barn were the ones I'd walked through— evil rooms, disgusting rooms. It was all some kind of trick.

That word "trick" got stuck in my head. A trick. All a trick. And I knew with a shock that made me dizzy that this whole thing had been set up. In a second, I understood that nothing I'd been told was real. There was no club house. No couch. No medal hanging on a nail. It was all made up. That story about Del sticking his knife in Will Hayes's mouth at Hopkins Park was made up. I'd just heard from Jamie that Will was at the party having a good time—not hiding from Del, not scared for his life. Then I had a terrible thought: Del *wanted* me to believe Will had left East Liberty because that's who was coming to the barn, it'd be Will the bulldozer—someone I wouldn't expect. Marty wouldn't bother phoning if Will left the party—he'd only call if Del left.

Just as I opened the door to run back through to the outside—to Danh and Jamie and our bikes and safety—I heard voices. I shut the door and snapped off my flashlight. The voices got louder and nearer: two men arguing. Not Will. But probably worse than Will. I felt like my feet had got nailed to the floor, and my heart started pounding so fast I thought I would black out.

"It's no big deal," one voice said, low and gravelly. "Just forgot to lock up. No one ever comes round here. Don't make a big deal of it. The key was where it was supposed to be."

"Christ it stinks," the other voice said. This one sounded more familiar—high pitched, nasal. "Can't you air this place out?"

"You never air out because you don't want no one to smell it," the first voice replied. "No one on the outside." He laughed. "You never did like getting your hands dirty. It was always me did the dirty work."

I crouched, keeping one eye against the keyhole for whatever I might see in the dark kitchen, until the ceiling fluorescents blazed on, like lightning that wouldn't stop. I jerked my head back. A minute later I was staring through the keyhole at Fulton Blake limping around in red flannel shirt and jeans, and Jamie's dad Hank Peterson in pressed trousers and a crew neck sweater, his face pinched and stern and ghostly white. He looked like he'd walked into the last place on earth where he wanted to be.

"I don't like it," Peterson said. "You should have replaced that dog that got shot. That door should have been locked. Check around carefully. Is everything exactly as you left it? Could one of your meth heads have broken in? Could your boy have been snooping around? I don't trust that boy of yours."

"It's all good. I told you, I just forgot to lock the door. Del knows not to come in. And he knows to mind me. I gave him a good lesson a couple nights ago. Everything's the same as always in here, so stop your worrying."

"You told me Boland came to your house."

"He came by the house but nowheres near the barn. He didn't see nothing. He was going on about Del and that prick Mathew Lyle. That's all he cared about—kid stuff. So I paid Lyle a visit. He won't be calling the cops again." Blake laughed a forced laugh.

"The thing is, now you're on Boland's radar," Peterson said. "I know what I'm talking about. You get on a cop's radar, no matter the reason, and it's time to pack it in. Knowing when to pack it in is how you survive. We had a good run, made a few bucks. Now we'll shut down, and do it fast. That's the only reason I'm here. We need to get rid of every scrap of this operation."

"I told you. No one's been in. Everything's fine."

"I'm not kidding," Peterson said. "We're shutting down."

When Del's dad started talking again, he was angry.

"You've got your big-ass store. Your bank account. People on your payroll. You think you're the boss. On the goddamn chamber of commerce. You know what I got? All's I got is what's here. This here's my bank account. I'll shut down, but I'm not dumping this batch. We cook this last batch, then we're done."

"The store doesn't make me a penny."

"We cook this batch, then we're done. That's what I'm saying. This is the last. I know what I'm doing now, so this'll be the biggest and the best. Everything's set to go."

He twisted the knob on the electric frying pan.

"Don't start that up," Peterson said. "It'll take too long. We don't have the time."

"You're not my boss," Blake said, turning to Peterson. "You're my kid cousin who's every bit as lowlife as me. I know what you've done. I know your history, every nickel you stole before you ran off from East Liberty, so don't tell me what to do. You never come down here where the real work is done. You don't like the *stink*. Don't like the *dirt*. Don't like to *pollute* yourself. Got your New York City nose in the air, don't you? Don't worry, you get used to the stink and shit and dirt pretty quick. There's a hell of a lot of it in East Liberty."

Blake turned back to the frying pan and the stove. Peterson grabbed his arm, but Blake shoved him away. "Fuck you," Blake yelled, and lunged for the shotgun in the corner. "I've fucking had enough of you." Peterson got hold of the barrel, and they started shoving and shouting "you bastard let go" and "I'll fucking kill you" while jerking in and out of my keyhole view. When they bumped into the shelf holding the bottles, I heard a crash and loud pop. Flames shot out of the frying pan. Peterson pried the gun away from Blake and slammed the barrel against the side of his head. When Blake slumped to the floor, Peterson stood still for a few seconds, as if he'd forgotten how to move, and just watched flames spread up the wall and across the floor. He kicked Blake in the stomach but Blake didn't move. Then flames began licking Blake's arm, leaping onto his sleeve—but he still didn't move. Peterson dropped the gun and started screaming "Fuck, fuck, fuck, fuck" while backing away, up against the door. He whipped around and ran through.

I flung open my door, grabbed the old winter coat off its hook, and threw it over Blake to smother the flames. I tried to lift Blake to his feet, telling him, "We gotta get outta here" and "I can't carry you," over and over, but he didn't respond. His head flopped around, as if his neck had stopped working. His clothes were smoking. I grabbed under his armpits and dragged him through the open door to the room with those hung-up deer that stunk of blood and guts, and kept on dragging, knocking over the bucket of deer organs, dragging Blake until I got us outside.

There for a few seconds I sat down next to Blake and caught my breath. I could see his pickup in the driveway and for a crazy moment wondered if I could somehow drive him to a hospital—though I'd only driven my dad's car once, around the Walmart parking lot. "Are you dead?" I screamed at the body. "Are you dead or alive?" A sudden, massive crackling and a blast of heat and smoke through the barn door got me up and yanking Blake along another ten yards. But that was it. I couldn't go further. My hands had cramped up and my legs turned to rubber. I guess to that point I'd been drawing on some kind of adrenaline rush.

Now I couldn't move a finger, let alone the two of us. And Blake was all dead weight. A fierce wall of heat blasted my face, chest, hands—but I didn't care. I felt it but didn't feel it.

I dropped to my knees and stared stupidly at the barn, knowing that the whole structure could explode at any second, chunks of flaming wood raining down on me and Blake. It didn't matter. I wasn't going anywhere. For the first time I looked closely at Fulton Blake's illuminated face. Red sores covered his lips and forehead. An ugly welt had puffed up where he'd been hit with the gun barrel. But strangely, he didn't look scary. He didn't look evil. He looked relaxed, almost like he was relieved to be unconscious or even dead. Relieved to have someone dragging his dead weight around. Then he jerked his head and gasped, sucking a breath. He was still alive.

A hand touched my shoulder, and though the touch terrified me because it could have been Will or Del or Peterson, I couldn't react, couldn't turn around. I didn't care what happened next. I was finished with caring, finished with everything. Then Danh's face appeared in front of my face, his mouth open, wide-eyed.

"You've got to get away from the barn!" he shouted. "Now!" He jumped behind me and locked his arm around my chest—Danh, scrawnier than me and a lot shorter, Danh actually lifted me up. Something about Danh showing his own strength got my strength flowing back, and we each put a hand under one of Blake's armpits, and together heaved him along the grass another thirty yards.

"Good enough," I said, panting.

I was about to ask Danh where Jamie was when two police cars raced from the road into Blake's long driveway, their white, red, and blue lights flashing, and I heard a fire engine siren start up in the distance.

"Let's get behind those trees," I told Danh, pointing to a line of evergreens. "They'll take care of Blake."

We ran into the darkness behind the evergreens, and Danh and I peeked around a thick trunk to watch Jack Boland, lit up by the burning barn, step out of the first patrol car. He shined his big flashlight around, caught sight of Blake's body, then sprinted back to his car. A minute later he was kneeling next to Blake with a first aid kit, checking his pulse. Meanwhile, fat old Daryl Monde hauled himself out of the second patrol car, walked a few steps towards what was left of the barn, and stared at the flames like he was watching a movie. A white van with *Madison County Drug Task Force* painted on it screeched in next, and four guys in white suits and gas masks jumped out, sprinting towards the fire but stopping short when a huge gushing noise erupted—the barn collapsing into hunks of burning wood and shooting flames, an arc of sparks like a terrifying version of East Liberty's Fourth of July fireworks. That's when the fire engine arrived.

"Jamie and I saw them," Danh whispered, beads of sweat glistening across his forehead. "We saw Del's dad and Jamie's dad each drive in. We watched them walk together to the barn."

Danh didn't seem scared at all, which surprised me. His voice was quiet and even.

"Jamie saw them too?"

"Yeah. We thought it was good that her dad was here. And then her dad ran out and drove away, and we saw flames and smoke. That's when Jamie called 911."

"Where's she now?"

"After we watched you drag out Del's dad, she took off running. I guess she just freaked out. You know, seeing her dad. Seeing him run away by himself."

"Poor Jamie," I said.

"That Blake guy would have died in there," Danh said. "I watched you drag him out. Just like your grandfather when he earned his medal. I should have run to help you, but I was too afraid."

"You saved him and me both," I said. "You arrived just in time. And you're strong for a little guy."

Danh and I watched the firemen do their work.

"That's got to be the biggest fire I'll ever see," Danh said. Then questions poured out. "Why was Jamie's dad here? What were they doing in that barn? Did Peterson start the fire on purpose? What was exploding in there?"

But I couldn't answer. I was just starting to figure out what questions to ask.

An ambulance charged into the driveway, and two men with a stretcher ran to Blake and Boland. I saw Boland wipe his forehead with a handkerchief as the men carried Blake to the ambulance. For some reason, maybe a cop's instinct, he suddenly turned and looked at me—directly into my eyes. I jerked my head behind the tree.

"Why did I have to look?" I whispered to Danh. "Why couldn't I just hide?"

"Come out from behind that tree," Boland shouted. "Right now. Come on out so I can see you. Put your hands above your head.

When I peeked around at him, I saw he'd drawn his gun.

———

A few minutes later, Danh and I were shivering in the back of a patrol car. I told Boland about the fight between Jamie's dad and Fulton Blake, about everything else I saw in the barn. He wrote lots of what I said in a little notebook. Danh told him how I'd dragged Blake out of the barn after the fire started.

"OK," Boland said, stuffing the notebook in his jacket pocket. "You two stay here." And he left to talk with Daryl Monde.

"Officer Monde will drive you home," Boland said when he returned. "Tomorrow, I'll need to talk with you both again. This is very serious." He turned to me. "That was a stupid thing you did, going in that barn by yourself. Stupid and dangerous."

"I know," I said.

"All right. Let's get you home."

"What about our bikes?" Danh asked.

"Get them in the morning."

"Jamie Peterson was with us too," I said, realizing I hadn't mentioned her. "But she left when she saw her dad leave. I'm worried about her."

"I'm going to the Peterson house right now," Boland said. "Hey," he said next. "What's that?" He shined his flashlight on my right hand. "Hold it up."

I raised my hand and in the light could see dime-size blisters across the skin.

"You got burned," he said. "And it needs attention."

I nodded.

"Jesus, why didn't you say something?"

The truth is, I hadn't felt pain while dragging Blake from the barn, or even while we hid behind the evergreens. But as soon as I held the hand up and examined it, I started feeling pinpricks, then a stinging that spread from the back of my hand to my wrist.

"Officer Monde will take you to the emergency room right now. I'll call your dad and tell him to meet you there."

He set a hand on my shoulder. "Dragging Fulton Blake out of that barn saved his life," he told me. "It was a brave thing to do."

I stared down at my blistered hand. I didn't know what to say.

———

Dad found me in a waiting room staring at the TV, though I couldn't have told him what I was watching. His face was pasty white, and stern, the two furrowed frown marks as deep as I'd ever seen them. After he looked over my bandaged-up right

hand, he left to find the doctor who'd worked on me. I kept staring at whatever flickering images I was watching, people on some
game show, laughing while music played and numbers lit up on
a board.

"What happened to you?" a voice asked—an old lady I hadn't
noticed before, in a chair across the lounge. Her gray hair was
perfectly permed, and she wore a blue old-lady dress with dark
stains down the front, and black, heavy shoes.

I held up my bandaged hand. "Got burned."

She nodded. "My boy . . ." She hesitated. "My boy got cut up,"
she said. She let loose a big moan. Her head dropped forward,
and her shoulders began shaking. She was twisting a little white
handkerchief around and around. "He called me, and I found
him. Why not 911?" she said. "Why me?"

"I guess he needed you," I said.

I walked over and sat next to her.

"His neck." She sobbed out the words. "He won't say who. But
I know, I know who in that bad crowd."

"What did the doctor say?" I asked.

"That he lost too much blood. That's what the doctor said,
'too much,' and wouldn't say more." And she started moaning and
crying again.

That's when I realized what had stained her dress.

I reached for her hand with my good hand. The handkerchief
was soaking wet.

Then Dad walked in the lounge, and I stood.

"Let's go," he said.

I said goodbye to the old lady, and Dad and I walked to the
parking lot, neither of us talking. My chatterbox Dad, my take-
charge Dad, with no words. He walked a little ahead of me.

"New tires," I said for no reason when we reached the car. I
kicked one.

"That's right," Dad said brusquely, then walked around to the driver's side and fished keys out of his pocket.

"Del Blake took Grandpa's medal," I said. "I didn't tell you about it. I couldn't. I'm sorry. I can't explain why."

Dad didn't say anything. He was leaning forward in the dark, trying to fit the key into the lock.

I wobbled, bracing myself on the hood to keep from falling. "I couldn't," I said again, this time sobbing out the words. "I just couldn't tell you. I couldn't. I couldn't."

I felt myself slipping.

Then Dad was next to me, his arms around me, propping me up. And it all gushed out, right in the dimly lit parking lot.

"When Mom called, she told me she wants to come home but doesn't want to be with you. I almost tried to kiss Jamie. Del's dad tortured him on a kitchen chair, even burned him with a cigarette. Del's girlfriend is too bizarre for words. I saw her wandering drunk and high near our house but didn't tell you. She wants something from me but I don't know what. Del thinks he's somehow my twin brother. Tommy tricked me into going into that barn. Will was part of it. Jamie's dad and Del's dad were cooking up drugs in a freaky kitchen. The purple martins had a mansion on a pole and now it's wrecked. In school kids are messing with Nazi stuff. There's real Nazis beating people up. I thought Will was coming to get me in the barn. What Grandpa wrote in his diary about that girl was like a dream I had once. I've been thinking about little Mike. I went to his grave by myself. I can't stop thinking that if I'd been a light sleeper, I would have woken up. I would have called you, and he might have lived. He must have made noise. He must have cried. I didn't want him to die—you've got to believe that. I wish I didn't have any of this in my head. There's too much crammed inside. Danh is OK. He helped me drag Del's dad from the barn. Del's got a knife, the knife his grandfather used to stab his dead wife. The knife he killed people with in Vietnam. Del must've stole it from his dad just like I stole the medal from your drawer. Gerald's letter was in a drawer. And Mom's letters to you. I've been lying about all kinds of things. Lying to you. Lying to everyone. Even my friends. I can't believe I've got real friends. But Jamie. . . ."

"OK," Dad said. "OK. It's OK."

He opened the door and eased me onto the seat. I don't remember the ride home. I don't remember how Dad got me into the house. But I remember at some point sipping hot chocolate at the kitchen table. I must have been awake, because I had the steaming white mug in my hand. But it was like I'd woken up just then. Dad was across from me. He wasn't angry. He was—it's hard to describe—he was looking at me like he used to a long time ago.

I set my head on my crossed arms, and conked out at the table. Next thing I knew, Dad was lifting me. He half-carried me up the stairs to my room, his arm around my waist. Dad folded back the bedcovers, and I sat on the edge, my head bent, my arms limp between my knees. He untied and loosened the laces, then pulled off my running shoes and socks. I flexed my toes, and then, in that half-conscious state, realized that something was different in my room. Something smelled different. It hit me: clean sheets. Dad had taken off the old sheets and put on ones he'd washed and dried, and made my bed. I'd never before smelled sheets that good.

"Grandpa's diary," I said, lifting my head. "You changed my bed. So you found it."

"I should have told you about that diary a long time ago. I thought I was protecting you."

"Grandpa didn't do anything to that girl, did he?" I lifted the covers and eased myself under.

Dad thought for a second. "In Berlin?"

I nodded.

"I don't know. I don't know everything that happened, or what was in his mind."

"But Grandpa was a hero. He won the Medal of Honor."

"Yes," Dad said, "he was a hero, no question."

I could tell he wanted to say something more but had trouble getting it out.

"You know . . . I mean . . . the bullet that killed him," he finally said. "It was from an M1. An American rifle."

"The sniper was our guy?"

"When Ollie Johnston told me my dad got killed in an off-limits black market by a bullet from an American rifle, I started to think . . . I don't know if he was shot for being a good guy or for being a bad guy. Or for hanging out with bad guys."

"It wasn't random?"

"Probably not. But we'll never know."

"How come you never told me?"

Dad shook his head. "I thought it was too complicated. I was wrong."

Complicated? I knew that war was complicated from all the war games I'd played since I was a kid, and then all the real strategies and campaigns I'd read about in books. But it turned out more complicated than I'd ever imagined, with what Grampa did in Berlin, what happened to Danh's dad in Vietnam, what Mr. Horn knew about Vietnam and Auschwitz that made him so angry he could hardly speak, and now these American Nazis beating up a teacher in East Liberty. I felt like I'd been through a war myself, in school and in that barn. It was all so complicated it made my head ache.

I don't remember saying goodnight. I don't remember Dad turning out the light or leaving my room. I slept in the clothes I was wearing, but Dad had pulled the covers to my neck.

I slept until morning without waking. I had dreams, but remembered only one:

I sat on a chair in the living room, Dad was on the couch holding little Mike in his lap. Mike was crying—maybe he was hungry and Mom wasn't home. Dad stood and paced back and forth across the room, singing lyrics from John Hiatt's "Lipstick Sunset" to little Mike. Then he sat down again on the couch with Mike on his lap. And they both fell asleep.

12

Saturday and Beyond

I WOKE UP LATE, almost ten o'clock, surprised to see that instead of a hand at the end of my right arm, there was a clump of white bandages. Then my hand began stinging so bad under the bandages it felt like the skin was getting burned all over again. The doctor had warned me that the body goes into shock when you first get burned, and it's a day later, when the shock and pills wear off, that the real pain starts up. And that pain can feel worse than actually getting burned.

Snapshots of the previous night appeared and disintegrated in my head like scenes from a Halloween horror movie: gutted deer, buckets of blood and organs, greasy pots and pans, Mr. Peterson's pinched face framed by the keyhole, as if he existed only inside that shape. I lay still for ten minutes, letting those snapshots form and fade, then slowly got myself up and out of bed, careful not to brush my throbbing, bandaged hand against anything. I wondered about the stink of smoke and cat piss in my room—until I realized it was me that stunk: my clothes, my hair, my skin.

Downstairs, Dad was on the phone with Jack Boland. It occurred to me that even after a big event like the fire at Blake's farm, and the stories that would be all over the newspaper and TV, people in this town would still sleep through the night, wake up, eat breakfast, use the bathroom, make phone calls, get on with their day. Even me. Somehow I would get on with my day.

Dad hung up the phone. Then he pressed a button so the phone wouldn't ring.

"Good morning!" he sang out.

Is he cheerful? I thought. Is that possible?

"How's the hand?"

"It hurts." I wanted to add "like hell" but caught myself.

"Why'd you turn the phone off?" I asked.

"Reporters are calling every five minutes. And a Channel 5 TV crew parked their van outside our house at six this morning wanting an interview, but I told them you were sleeping. They said they'd come back."

"I don't want to talk to anyone," I said.

"That's fine," Dad said. "I'll keep them away."

He brought me two pills on a saucer, and a glass of water. "You'll be taking these every six hours for the pain. Wednesday, I'll bring you in to get the dressing changed, and they'll do an evaluation."

"Am I going to school?"

"Not until the doctor says it's OK."

That was a relief. All I wanted was to lie on the couch. I didn't want to see anyone. Didn't want to do anything.

"Breakfast in two shakes," Dad said. "Pancakes, bacon, eggs, anything you want."

"Dad," I said.

He turned to me.

"When you picked me up at the hospital, I was pretty out of it, wasn't I?"

"Yes," Dad said. "You were."

"What did I say? You know, in the parking lot."

"What did you say? Everything." He smiled and shook his head. "You said everything you could think of."

While cooking, Dad started humming a tune, then sang some words: "Wake up, wake up on a Saturday night." I let out a few snorts, but soon laughed right out loud.

"What's so funny?" Dad asked.

"It's Hilary Duff. That's what you're singing."

"Who's she?"

"You don't need to know. I don't even need to know."

"OK," he said. "I probably don't. Listen, today we're getting you cleaned up. Seriously cleaned up. You stink."

"I know," I said. "Believe me, I know."

He brought over my plate of food, sat down, cut everything up, and started feeding me. I opened my mouth like a little bird while Dad put in forkfuls—I was starving. While I ate he told me what he'd found out from Jack Boland: Del's dad was badly burned, but he came to consciousness at the hospital. Boland then charged him with drug trafficking and a dozen violations for the toxic stuff he'd used to cook his drugs. Boland even got him for hunting deer off-season. He arrested Peterson at his home, in his chair in the family room, watching TV as if he was just a normal person in a normal house.

I could now see the why and the how of everything that had happened. Del was the real chess master. Del was the general who manipulated his toy soldiers, setting them here and there as needed. He knew what his dad was doing in that barn. He'd gotten Tommy to talk me into going there just before his dad would come home. It was his way of getting back at his dad for the life he was given and back at me for . . . well, for being me. But he didn't factor in Danh and Jamie. He didn't factor me in either—not completely.

Del had planned every detail, including his escape. He disappeared from East Liberty, along with his Grand Prix—I guess he was able to drive with one arm in a sling. Later, I found out that Vera had gone with him, though nobody except me seemed to notice. They just got into Del's car after the Hopkins Park party, started driving and never stopped. Poor Vera, I thought. She'd gone with Del because that was somehow better than staying at home—which makes you wonder, what could home have been like? And why was being alone not possible? She had nowhere else to go, no one else who would tell her she really was a person who breathed in and exhaled. She must have thought she didn't exist unless Del told her so. What could she have been thinking that night, next to Del in the front seat of his Grand Prix, racing down dark country roads leading God knows where? What would her life be like from now on? And how long would it last?

Boland wasn't sure how involved Del had been in making and selling crystal meth. Maybe not at all, though he certainly knew it was going on. And whether or not he used meth, he definitely gave it to his friends. I wondered if Del took my grandpa's medal with him when he drove out of East Liberty that night. But I didn't really care. I didn't want to see that medal ever again. It could hang around Del's neck everywhere he went for all I cared, along with all the baggage of who hurt him, and who he needed to hurt back for reasons I'm glad I can't understand. It could nest forever in the tobacco tin next to the scalp and hair of the nameless Vietnamese boy, a year older than me if Del was telling the truth, who may himself have been a killer, or as innocent as Danh—or something in between.

"Jack Boland wants to talk with you this afternoon," Dad said when I'd finished breakfast. "He needs to go over everything one more time. When he's done, we should do something. Maybe get some takeout from Salvatore's. Isn't their pizza better than Domino's? What d'you think?"

"I'm supposed to go to Rusty's to watch baseball. The game starts at noon."

"You're not doing that," Dad said. "You're staying home today."

"Yeah," I said. "OK."

To tell the truth, staying home was exactly what I wanted to do.

"Oh," I said. "Reverend Haroldson called. I forgot to tell you. You're having dinner with her tonight."

"I'll cancel," Dad said.

"No. You should go. She's nice. A little out of touch, but nice. I'll be fine. I'll watch TV."

Dad laughed. "No, I'll reschedule."

"I want you to go."

Dad was surprised. "Really? Even if she's a little—how did you put it?—out of touch?"

"Yeah," I said. "But so are you." I paused. "I mean in a good way. You two sort of match in out-of-touch-ness."

"Still," he said, "I'll reschedule."

Dad followed me upstairs to my bedroom to help me get into clean clothes. It was awkward. We didn't talk while he pulled off my sweatpants and helped me get on fresh underwear, socks, and jeans. We didn't look at each other. Then we had to think about which T-shirt, shirt, or sweater had a sleeve wide enough for my bandaged hand.

"I've got just the thing," Dad said.

He left and a minute later walked in holding his cardigan, the one he was wearing on our Sunday walk when this whole thing started.

"It's clean. You don't have to pull it over your head. The sleeves are extra wide. It's warm. Like a big, fuzzy shirt."

I stared at him. He was serious.

"You want me to wear that? I can't. That's . . . that's just disgusting."

Then he laughed, long and hard, right there in my bedroom. He was laughing so hard he dropped the cardigan and doubled over. I have to say, he pulled it off pretty well. He even got me laughing about that stupid cardigan. That day I ended up wearing one of Dad's oversize flannel shirts, which he buttoned up for me.

———————

Saturday evening Dad and I watched the TV news version of what happened at the Blake farm, with footage of smoldering wreckage that used to be the barn. A girl reporter interviewed Jack Boland, who told how Bernie Schill had tipped him off about the barn meth lab, which explained how he and the Drug Task Force got there so fast. He said meth from that lab was being sold all over the county—even in schools. When the reporter described "Justin Lyle, the fifteen-year-old who dragged Fulton Blake out of the burning barn, saving his life," that person didn't seem to be me but a kid who happened to look like me. They showed footage of my house, and my dad at the front door waving reporters away.

Monday evening I phoned Danh to fill him in on what I'd learned about Blake and Peterson getting arrested, and Del leaving town with Vera. I told him my burns would keep me out of school for a while.

"Is Jamie back?" I asked.

"She's back. She was in school today."

"Really? She didn't miss a day? How is she?"

"She looks fine."

"What do you mean 'looks fine'? Did she say anything about what happened?"

"I haven't talked to her."

"Have you tried?"

Danh was quiet. "Not really. I passed her in the hall, and she didn't see me. She seemed . . . busy. When did you say you're coming back to school?"

"I don't know," I said. "As soon as Dad lets me."

I next phoned Jamie's cell, but it rang twenty times without a recording or being picked up. Then I tried her home phone, but hung up when the answering machine clicked on: I didn't want to hear her Mom's chirpy voice telling me to "Please leave a detailed message. . . ."

———

I didn't go out of the house until my Wednesday doctor's appointment—Dad wanted to be sure the burns were healing up, with no sign of infection. My hand had started itching like crazy, which Dad said was a good thing. So I mostly read books from Dad's library, or watched TV, or stared out my bedroom window at the autumn leaves falling, the squirrels running along branches with nuts in their mouths, getting ready for winter. Dad cooked a breakfast for me every morning, and came home to make me lunch and dinner. I'm not sure how he got all his teaching done. Mom called every day. When I first told her the story of what happened, she said she was flying back to see me, but I convinced her that it wasn't a big deal. I was fine, just bandaged up some. Then she sounded angry. How could this happen? Didn't my father monitor where I was? How could I be foolish enough to go by myself into a stranger's barn at night? Especially the barn of a guy as awful as Fulton Blake? Once all that was out of the way, she got teary and choked up, telling me how much she loved me, how worried she was, how she couldn't bear the thought of anything bad happening to me. Was I getting enough medical attention, did I want to fly to San Diego and stay with her for a while? Gerald, she said, would be happy to pay for the flight.

My first thought was: are you kidding? San Diego? Gerald? But behind that thought was another thought or, I guess, another feeling. It came on suddenly how much I wanted to see her, to be with her, not just talk on the phone.

"Can I visit over Christmas vacation?" I said. "That's not too far away. I mean, if it's OK with Dad."

"That would be great," Mom said. "Really great. I miss you so much."

"I miss you too," I said.

"Are things better?" I asked. "I mean, with Gerald?"

She was quiet. "A little," she said. "I think a little better."

———

On Wednesday a nurse cut off the bandages, examined the skin, wrapped my hand in fresh bandages, and pronounced me "doing just fine." She said my dad could change the dressing from now on.

"But be prepared," she added. "When it's healed, there'll be scars. We'll do everything we can to minimize scarring, but it's part of the process. OK?"

"OK," I said. I shook my head to clear out a vision of a red spider web stitched across my hand.

"When am I going back to school?" I asked.

"Stay home through the weekend," she said. "You can go on Monday if your father is satisfied with how you're healing when he changes the dressing."

"There's one good thing about your burned hand," Dad said.

"What's that?"

"You won't have to do dishes for a while. Or clean your room."

That struck me as pretty funny, and my laughing got Dad laughing, and we sat in that little examination room laughing like two lunatics, with the nurse staring at us, smiling a tight little smile.

———

I was nervous going to school after my week off, and most nervous about seeing Jamie. Ever since the night of the barn fire

I'd wanted to talk with her, to see how she was surviving her turned-around family: from daughter of a successful local businessman to daughter of a drug-dealing attempted murderer. I sent her an e-mail from Dad's computer, just a simple "How are you?" but got nothing back. I phoned her every night of the week, but no one picked up—it was always the machine.

Because of my bandaged hand, I couldn't ride my bike to school, and so I had to take the bus, which I hadn't done since last spring. I wished I'd asked Danh to ride with me, but with everything going on in my head, I just forgot. So that Monday morning I was by myself.

It was strange getting off the bus, hearing the *whoosh* of the door, filing down the metal steps to the curb with all the other kids, everyone but me shoving and yelling, streaming towards the school's front doors as if nothing had changed. Of course nothing had changed for them. But everything had changed for me. I could see it in the way teachers and students looked at me as I walked down the halls—or deliberately avoided looking at me. I'd become a different person from the one they knew, and they had to start figuring me out from scratch. Word must have buzzed around school all week about the fire at the Blake barn and the drug bust and arrests. No one could know the full details, or why I was even at the barn. But they'd learned enough from the TV and newspaper.

On my way to homeroom that first Monday morning back, I saw Danh pulling books out of his locker and ran over, shouting his name. But when he turned, he just stood there, a blank expression on his face. Even though we'd talked on the phone every night, in person he was wary, waiting to see what I'd do, to find out how everything that happened had changed our friendship. I grabbed his thin shoulder with my good hand and shook him. "We're OK!" I told him. "It's all over. We did it."

I didn't know what to say next, but words just came out. They weren't meant as bragging, though anyone who overheard might think so.

"We're heroes," I said. "You and me together. We're heroes." And he smiled.

After homeroom, I had to catch my breath when I saw Jamie walking down the hall—the first time I'd seen her since the night we biked to the Blake barn. I wasn't surprised to see her—that had to happen some time. I was surprised that she was walking with my friend Rusty. He was talking fast, and gesturing with both hands. She held her head high and stared straight ahead as she walked. She wouldn't look at me. It's not like she couldn't see me, staring at her wide-eyed, my stump of a right hand so bandaged up it was a big red flag at the end of my arm. But Rusty craned his head toward me as he passed, still talking fast and loud at Jamie, and gave me a big wink.

During lunch Danh and I ate together at our old table, and I saw Jamie a few tables away with Rusty across from her, just the two of them. Rusty was still talking, Jamie was still silent, poking at her salad with a fork.

"Did you talk with her yet?" Danh asked. "You must have, right? Tell me you talked with her."

I didn't answer. I looked at Danh, frowning at me, then over at Jamie. I stood and walked straight to her table.

Rusty saw me first. "Hi Justin." He acted as if sitting at a lunch table alone with Jamie and me walking over with a big bandage on my hand was the most normal thing in the world.

"Hi Rusty."

Jamie put down her fork.

"I don't mean to interrupt," I said to both of them. Then to Jamie: "Can we talk some time?"

I glanced at Rusty, smiling at the two of us.

"Rusty," she said, speaking slowly. "Are you thirsty? I'm really thirsty."

"Yeah," Rusty said. "Me too. Definitely. Why don't I get us some Cokes?" And he stood up. "Justin," he said. "How about you?"

"No, I'm good, thanks."

I sat in the chair next to Jamie. "I've been worried," I said. "How are you?"

"I'm OK. Thanks. Thanks for asking." She took a deep breath. "I read your e-mail. I know you've been trying to call. I should have called you. Your hand got burned, didn't it?" She lightly touched my bandaged hand, but pulled back quickly. "How does it feel?"

"Not too bad," I said. "It hurts less every day."

"I couldn't call," Jamie said. "I couldn't." She said those words haltingly, as if it was painful just to talk. "I can't do much of anything. I can hardly get out of bed in the morning."

I glanced over at Rusty, stuck in a line at the soda dispenser. "And Rusty?" I said.

"He's sort of been around. You know, hanging around. He's nice. I don't have to talk much."

I laughed a little, and for a moment she actually smiled.

"I'm sorry," she said, serious again. "I'm just . . . really sorry."

Suddenly I didn't care about Rusty, or that Jamie had walked past me in the hall, seeing me but not seeing me. Something was wrong. She didn't sound right. Her voice had gotten flatter, quieter. She didn't even have the energy to brush off Rusty.

"It's OK," I said. "I mean, we're talking now."

"I'm going away," Jamie said next, staring down at her salad.

"What do you mean?"

"We're leaving East Liberty."

"Your whole family?"

She nodded. "Mom doesn't want to be in town while the legal stuff is happening. She doesn't have any real friends here anyway.

And the store's closed now. We'll stay with Mom's sister in White Plains, and I'll go to school there for a while. Dad . . . Dad's lawyer is based in Brooklyn."

And I wondered, what could the Peterson family dinners be like now? And what on earth is her brother Tony doing?

"Will you come back?" I asked.

"I'm not sure. I'm not sure of anything right now."

"Do you want to go?"

"I don't know what I want. But I'm going."

"When do you leave?"

"Tomorrow morning. I'll get out of school early today to help pack, so I'll miss history. I'll call Danh tonight to tell him."

"He's right over there," I said, tilting my head towards Danh, staring at us from his table.

"I know," she said. "But I can't right now. Please try to understand."

She took hold of my good hand and squeezed it, which made me remember when I held that old lady's hand in the hospital waiting room. "I'm doing what I have to do," she said, letting go.

Then Rusty was back with two full soda cups.

"Long line," he said. "Took forever. And they're out of Coke. Why do they always run out of Coke? I think there's an anti-Coke conspiracy in this school."

Good old Rusty, I thought. Good old clueless Rusty. Happy as can be to be sitting at a lunch table with East Liberty's hottest, nicest, smartest girl, even if she is the daughter of a criminal. Happy to be complaining about the soda dispenser. Happy to be my friend. I felt this welling up inside. I don't know what to call it—I guess just feeling good that guys like Rusty are around.

"So what's happening?" Rusty said to me.

"Nothing much. I've got to go actually. Haven't even eaten."

"Come to my house next Saturday," Rusty said. "You and Danh, OK? The Mets are playing. Fred will be there."

"OK," I said. "See you then."
"Goodbye Justin," Jamie said.
And I said goodbye.

————

Back at the table with Danh, I had a thought—a simple thought, which was this: there are reasons why things happen.

There are reasons why that squirrel on the roadside back when this all started had to die. And reasons why Tommy had to throw that cup of piss out the window at my dad. And reasons why Del hated his dad, and hated me, and wanted to hurt both of us. Reasons why Vera had to disappear and leave no trace, as if she'd never sat at a cafeteria table, never walked down a school hall, never took hold of my hand by my locker. Reasons why Danh and I became friends. Reasons why my hero Grandpa had to get shot by a G.I. in a Berlin black market. Reasons why he wasn't a perfect hero. Reasons why Mom fell out of love with Dad, and in love with Gerald, and out of love again. Reasons why my brother had to die before he could even live. And reasons why Jamie hated her father, and needed a boy to talk to her and walk with after her father got arrested. And reasons why that boy couldn't be me.

Here's the thing about those reasons: some you can figure out, some you can accept, and some just remain a mystery.